Wildflower

Published by the Great Unpublished company.
Printed in the United States of America.

Wildflower

Carl Rafala

greatunpublished.com
Title No. 98
2000

Wildflower

ACKNOWLEDGMENTS:

"Boxboy" first appeared as "Boy in a Box" in Twilight Times, January 2000.

"The Invisible War" first appeared in Twilight Times, October 1999.

CONTENTS

SOUL SOLUTION

1 Down Time

In the darkness there was hissing, the slow, steady sound of filtered air somewhere in the dark recesses of the Hole. Then the slight sucking of inhalation, a deep breath drawing in, out, in, out, slow, methodical, ceaseless, as if the very darkness that surrounded her was alive and breathing over her shoulder. It marked the seconds almost precisely, which helped her mark the minutes, and the minutes into hours which seemed to stretch on as long as the darkness was deep.

The only way to push back the encompassing black was when she moved, triggering a little green nano-firefly which winked on, creating a halo about a meter around her. A small bubble of cold, green light to hold back the night.

And from somewhere behind her came a whimper or groan. The only sounds that let Maria Osbourne know that she was still alive.

The interface still strapped to her temple, she could feel Piers pulling at her mind. She hesitated, then linked up and could see him in her helmet interface sitting on a virtual beach, toying with mechanical parts which floated in the air about his head, growling to himself. She shook off the spooky feeling she always got when she interfaced and for once felt a bit of relief. He was still functioning and outside the V-wing somewhere upon the cool ice and slush of

Titan, assessing the damage.

Their approach vector was cleared all the way to the habitat, but the shifting winds and mysterious turbulence which seemed to explode into existence from nowhere shook the sleek boomerang, ripping control thrusters from their moorings and warping the wing tips. The alarms had sounded. The flyer was going down.

She drew a deep breath of cool, dark air, remembered the screeching sound of the siren, the dung colored clouds swishing by, Anya wrestling with the controls. Then the nano-bugs wrapped them each in a luminescent web of finely spun threads and dragged them down into the crash Hole in the belly of the ship. Then her suit drugged her. The rest was merciful blackness.

There was movement behind her. A firefly winked on.

"Anya," she said. "Anya, you okay?"

"What happened?" came a raspy, dry voice. "Are we down?"

"Yeah, we're down. Down and out," she replied heavily. "Welcome to Titan."

Maria could hear a grunt and some shuffling. Anya testing her muscles. "Give me a run down. How's the ship? Are we in danger?"

"No immediate danger," said Maria. "The V-wing is a mess, though."

"What's Piers say?"

If Anya could see her glare "Thanks" at her in the dim light she would. Of all things she enjoyed interfacing with Piers the least. She drew a deep breath before she tapped into Piers' mind. She shuddered at the level of intimate contact. A three dimensional picture of the ship hovered before her in grid-space. Piers threw as much information at her as her brain could handle. "Main power in off-line and the hull has been breached in many quarters. Basically there's too much damage for Piers to handle. On the lighter side, *Cassini* should be coming out of darkside soon and run smack-dab into the distress siren. She'll make a course correction to come get us, pronto." She shook herself, as if bugs were crawling up her flesh.

"Awe, shit!" Anya murmured. "It'll be at least three, maybe four days before she makes it back from Saturn. *Cassini* doesn't use fusion boosters. She's a coaster ship, babe, uses basic chemical fuel for acceleration and then drifts along. We'll run out of air."

"Great!" Maria replied. "Well we can't sit here."

"How far are we from the target?"

The habitat had been sent ahead, automated with droids to erect the structure and tend to it six months before. *Cassini* was to perform a flyby of the inner moons and dip into the upper layers of Saturn's heavy cloud banks. Because Titan had swung outward in her orbit in comparison with *Cassini's* inward trajectory, she was too far away for immediate drop-off. In the interest of saving fuel, *Cassini* had dumped them by the outer moons and they had to fly their way in. After a fourteen month tour, *Cassini* would pick them up on their way out.

Six kilometers, said Piers from his virtual beach, blonde hair wriggling in a sea breeze.

"About six kilometers."

"We've got to get to the habitat and start her up." Anya started to get up. "In forty-three hours we'll need air. Now, let's pop this top and get outta here."

* * *

Maria stood upon the surface of frozen Titan.

The ship lay flat upon the ice in a trench dug by the sliding and grinding of the hull upon impact. They had emerged from a top hatch and climbed down. The emergency lights were on and glowed an eerie red, and the light was quickly swallowed barely six meters out by the absorbing haze, providing little comfort. Above, the deep dung colored clouds of nitrogen and hydrocarbon smog moved like a thick soup, with sudden surges curling across the sky. The temperature registered at 95 degrees Kelvin.

"Awe, shit!" Anya was exclaiming. "Would you look at that! I don't think the insurance is gonna cover that!"

The ethane mist floating through the air had clouded her vision. Maria reached up and wiped her helmet faceplate with her gloved hand. A bio-chem researcher for twenty-four years, this was her last field excursion before accepting a lectureship at Cambridge.

This is an interesting way to end my career, she mused, glancing at the wrecked V-wing.

"The company should have chartered a military ship," said Anya, scornfully. "Something heavy and bulky."

"Yeah, well, they didn't. And anyway, I thought you were suppose to be good!"

Anya looked up, eyes drawn sharp. "You need the right ship for the right conditions. Every good pilot knows *that*." She slid down from the top of the ship. "Damn it all!"

"You okay?"

"Yeah," she replied. "I just landed in something soft." Maria could hear her heaving as she walked out of it and around the nose of the ship. "Just some methane slush."

"Great. Care for a slushball fight?"

"Cute. Any news from Piers?"

Anya could never get comfortable with the link-up idea, and so left all the communication with the bio-bot to her. Many others felt the same way about interacting with the bots, the freakshows, as they were called. Maria thought it all rather macabre herself, but someone had to do it. On this mission, anyway.

Piers had once been an atmospheric scientist. After a crash on Callisto sixty years lost he was dying. Rather than having his damaged areas regrown he gave permission to expire and have his neural patterns downloaded into a bio-bot's main core, which was organically grown and maintained by nanos. He had become one of the thousands of humans impressed into bio-machines, where specially designed nucleic acids and replicated RNA mimic the higher brain functions. With access to any desired upgrade, they were able to learn any trade or profession in a nano-second. Unhindered by flesh, they could perform tasks Biologicals couldn't perform, or at least not as efficiently.

Debates leaned toward the notion that bio-bots were merely reflections, images of true Biologicals once impressed in human flesh, now uploaded into organically grown brains. Soulless information. The Theosophical Society of Ganymede felt otherwise, and pushed to secure them confederate rights. Life is defined by what it does, they protested. Its function creates a link, a sameness that binds all life together.

However the bio-bots were shunned by whatever societies they inhabited. Eventually they left Homeworld altogether. Most took up residence in the Jovian System.

Whatever the case, Maria still found it downright freaky speaking to a dead person.

The interface at her left temple pulsed with information, with Pier's voice-thoughts. Maria reluctantly touched a press-pad on her suit arm and linked up. "He says that long and short range communications are out. We've only got the automated distress beacon for now."

Anya glanced over at Piers. The bot's many arms and legs worked over the stern of the ship, probing, removing, analyzing. She thought she could feel the icy cold beyond her thermal suit and shivered. "Okay. First things first: salvage what you can from the ship and keep a check on *Cassini's* proximity beacon. I'll head out for the habitat and get her ready."

Maria nodded.

They salvaged what they could and lay everything, food stuffs, oxygen tanks, spare parts, side-by-side on the ice. Most of the research equipment, the things that didn't come with the habitat months earlier, were destroyed. What remained of the food and air was dangerously low, not enough to sustain them for a week, let alone a fourteen month stay.

Maria shook her head at the remaining chem-equipment. Not much that was useful was left. In her short time here she'd have to make do with what she had. Being a geologist as well as a pilot, Anya could had it much easier, and with a pick axe, seismic sensors and basic analyzing tools, she could produce more results than Maria.

Maria could only frown at the wreck for any lost opportunities.

Something moved past her. She started.

Anya came bounding around the side of the ship. "What is it?"

"I don't know...I..." she fell silent. Something glided past her field of vision. She jerked around. "Did you see it?"

"See what?"

The silence between them was heavy. Maria's gaze tried to penetrate the smog. "I...There!"

As they both turned a swarm of large white particles floated up and out from the haze straight at them. They were large, white and wispy, like dandelions gone to seed, carried on a summer's wind. They came from an easterly direction, behind the ship.

"What the hell..." Anya flinched at the fluff balls that bounced around off her suit.

Maria reached out and touched one, gingerly. It's filaments bent and sprung back as it landed in her open palm. She cupped her hand to prevent its escape. "Unbelievable," she whispered.

Suddenly the air was clear again. Nothing but haze around them.

"Anya, did we just see life?"

"I don't know. Did we?"

"We just saw life," Maria said. "On Titan."

Anya folded her arms across her chest. "Maria."

"There must be a delicate ecology here. Mars wasn't the only find!" She held the white fluffball in her hand like a precious piece of glass that could shatter if she moved to awkwardly.

"Could you hold on a moment."

Maria regarded her with her full attention for the first time. "What?"

Anya shuffled her feet. "Look," she said stiffly. "I'm all for this. You know I am. But let's not get sidetracked. Our ship is useless and our supplies are low. Right now survival is priority one. Okay? Hell we don't even have the proper equipment for this anymore."

"I know, but..." She had to record the event, make a preliminary examination at least. She could see Anya was uneasy.

"There might be time later. Right now I'd like to live." Anya said, placing her hand under Maria's.

Maria knew she was right, of course. But it didn't make it any easier to ignore this.

"Okay?"

Maria nodded. She looked down at the ball of fluff in her palm. Then Anya slowly lifted Maria's hand up and let the breeze carry it away.

2
The Face of Darkness

Anya assembled the rover while Maria stacked the supplies for loading. Anya would need to drive the supplies over to the habitat. It was the only vehicle they had, so Anya would have to make two, maybe three trips. And the rover's speed was painfully slow.

When it was completed and stocked up, Anya took the homing device, locked on to the habitat's signature beacon, and drove off into the haze, disappearing like a shadow behind a curtain. Maria continued pulling things out from inside the wreck, lamely.

If she finished too soon she'd have nothing to do but wait for Anya to return. She decided to take it slow. Better to have something to do rather than wait around here, alone. Or think about that fuzzy, as she now called it. The ice crunched under her feet as she stacked crates a few meters from the ship, and although the ground was solid enough she felt like a skater on untested ice, unsure, and so walked with carefully placed steps.

After going back into the Hole to change her air filter, she worked for almost an hour straight. She grew tired and stopped to rest where she was stacking crates, a few meters from the ship. She propped herself up against a boulder of ice. To say that the crash, unloading the ship, and the events of the past few hours sucked her energy dry would be spot on the money. It became even more difficult when another swarm of fuzzies glided by. She watched them tumbled and roll on a wind she couldn't feel. If she could only have some time...

Keep busy.

For the first time, feeling Piers at the back of her mind, she almost envied him. Never needed sleep or had to worry about hunger, air, going to the toilet, any of it. Out here, or indeed anywhere, he was totally self-sufficient and self-sustaining. It was what she needed if she were to conduct any kind of serious study in the short time she would be here.

For a brief moment there was a rip in the cloud blanket above. A single column of light shone down from the heavens outside and for a second she could see Saturn's rings, as if painted on the deep sky beyond.

She pushed herself up from against the frozen boulder and moved forward. Her feet sank down in what she thought was methane slush, but it pulled at her ankles. The light beam expanded, the icy surface exploded on in a blinding fury. She put her hands up to her faceplate. When her eyes adjusted she lowered them and proceeded to relieve herself in her suit. The recycler kicked in.

She was standing in the wake of a dark pool, wide and black as night. A pool of thick sludge with small tributaries, oozing over the surfaces like spilled ink. Then the rip in the clouds stitched itself shut, the light column thinned and disappeared, and the pool was gone.

In the foggy aura of her suit light she stared at the wall of haze before her.

She pulled herself out and heard a muffled slurping sound as her feet came clear of the muddy substance. The darkness stained her boots.

* * *

The light of day was receding (if the dung colored light which slithered through the hydrocarbon smog could truly be called light) and it was getting even more difficult to see. She had made several surveys of the pool, which stretched onward for several hundred meters, maybe more. She had also covered a good portion of ground around the area, to see if she could spot any more pools, gathering data as she went. There were unique crystallization effects in ranges of raspberry colored ice. But the most interesting discovery remained the dark pools of what Piers had confirmed was organic matter. And there were dark circles, micro-granules, floating in the thick substance.

Piers kept her company through the link, was monitoring through her suit cameras and accessing the data-pad she held in her hand. The bio-bot was not only working on bringing up the V-wing's reserve power grid for information download, but had also accessed ANALYSIS mode, beginning a preliminary probing of the sludge. Multiple task capability was such a plus side to being uplinked, and a bio-bot was standard an every vessel for those very obvious reasons.

Through their interfacing Pier's curious thoughts mingled with hers. Thoughts on the possibility of finding life in such a barren system, floated through her. Most of the earlier searches had turned up nothing, and the only other sign of life ever found anywhere was on Mars. But when it had finally been determined that small lifeforms, minute crustaceans, did live in the deep caverns of Mariner Valley, mining and development had already shattered their fragile little eco-system beyond repair.

Piers was on such an accelerated level of cognition that she found it hard to keep up with him, even to separate her thoughts from his. And with access to all areas of knowledge he was all things at once, pondered all things, considered, evaluated...

There is most definitely a large underground sea here, he related to her. Piers had had time to sink a few probes into the ground and was collecting the data. *There is a water sea under all this ice. Sludgy, of course, and mostly frozen in places, but it's there. That indicates the existence of an underground heat source. Possible some form of mild inner volcanism occurring.*

"But that dark matter is on the surface," she said. "There would need to be a concentrated heat source, like an impact or thermal venting, for these granules to exist. What about that? Could an impact or venting heat up the ice enough to create complex soups for a prolonged period, just long enough for organic life to form?"

For the soup to form, yes. But organisms beyond the single-celled? Doubtful. He scratched his head. *I've detected no signs of thermal venting of any kind, but that doesn't mean it hasn't happened. An impact sounds reasonable. A heavy particle cloud was discovered to dip into this area of Saturn's orbit on a regular basis. Add ultraviolet light to particle bombardment and organics could have formed in isolated pools. They would obviously die out when the area cooled.*

"And what about the fuzzies? How do they fit in?"

He didn't know. *They're carried on the wind currents. From where I don't know, but they appear to ingest the hydrocarbons. They use their filaments to suck it up, like straws.*

They eat this smog? she thought. And there was something else. As they floated they seemed to come up at her. *Up.*

"Any thoughts on their function? How do they fit into an eco-system?"

None. But again, that doesn't mean they don't have one. Maybe their function is to simply live.

Samples from deep under Titan's frozen wastes floated before her, and there were analysis of hydrocarbons, weather patterns, sludge composition. Her helmet's three dimensional projector was making the pictures shimmer with life. She catalogued the information for later use.

These granules are most certainly dead, if they were even alive at all. If we're to find anything alive it has to be underground.

"That underground sea is difficult to reach," Maria said flatly.

Maybe this time around. But that sea is water. If you want higher level organics that's a good place to start.

She cocked her head at the images, wondering what else was down there, elusive because she lacked the necessary equipment.

She sighed, feeling defeated.

* * *

"You'll wanna see the file."

"Seen it. Can't prove it yet," said Anya, heaving a box upon the rover, pausing to catch her breath. Anya had just made it back to the crash site when Maria called in from the pool several hundred meters downrange. Maria caught serious hell for being away.

"It's organic matter. Piers has made a thorough analysis on what we have so far, and it looks like multiple-celled organism."

Obviously Anya felt they had no time for this, and showed her annoyance. "Look, we're dying here. First order of business is survival. Can't do a proper job if you've stopped breathing."

"Or don't have the necessary equipment," said Maria. "I know. But I also know my job."

"The evidence for those granules being lifeforms is tenuous at best," said Anya heavily. "All you've got so far is a pool of inert organic compounds. You don't even know how it was formed in this cold."

"I can explain that last part pretty easily," Maria said. "A basic experiment. You take simple molecular compounds, such as the ones here on Titan, subject them to energy sources such as lightning, heat from impacts, and complex compounds associated with life forms and it creates a sludge-type mass. A late Twen-Cen scientist called it Tholin. That's Greek for muddy."

"Bully for him," Anya retorted. "So you have an organic soup. Okay. But these granules, the processes of a more complex, higher form functioning in this cold are problematic. And these fuzzies–"

There was a thud and a muffled cry.

"Anya." Maria stood frozen in the near darkness. "Anya! You okay?"

"Fine," she huffed. "Just fine."

"What happened?"

"I collapsed, is all," she said. "I'm tired and stressed out like hell. Look, it took forever to boot up the systems at the habitat. Then the enviro-unit developed a hiccup, twice, and the high gain needed parts replaced. Shit, the reactor itself took a while to kick in. Thought it was busted."

"Okay, just take it easy. I'll be done here soon and then I'll give you a hand."

"How thoughtful. But I'm gonna take this load over now. I'm sure you'll want to eat properly for the next few days. Then I'll come back and get you. If you're done playing around in the snow, that is."

"Thanks." Maria shook her head. Anya was too strong-willed for her own good sometimes. "If you're okay with that. Fine. Go without me," she snapped. She heard Anya suck in a mouthful of air.

"I was thinking," said Maria, carefully, "that maybe we could spare some supplies from Cassini, enough to carry us on at least half of our original fourteen month stay. She has some of the equipment I need. I'd be able to run more tests, a detailed analysis."

"Forget it," said Anya. "Not this time around. All the time tables are screwed now."

"But we can't just leave this!"

"You'll make a report on your preliminary findings. Piers will continue to gather data until pick-up. We're now reduced to recon. It will be the problem of the second team."

"Anya!"

"There are no ships scheduled to come back out this way for fourteen months. There'd be no one to pick us up when our supplies run out. One person might manage three months on what's left. But again, there's no transport. And they won't alter the time tables." She drew in air. "Sorry, babe. This one's a scrub."

"Anya!" Maria protested. "There has to be a way!"

"Just be at the crash site when I get back."

                              * * *

When Anya pulled up to the V-wing they hardly spoke to each other.

Maria was fidgeting with her data-pad, examining the samples and interfacing with Piers. He had finished his examination of the ship, had downloaded the central core, and was out drilling into the sludge pool nearby. It was almost completely dark; in a short while it would be pitch black. Maria had turned on the ship's headlights.

Anya loaded the last of the supplies onto the rover and made a final check of the ship for anything they might have overlooked. They're was. Maria noticed Anya's movements were quick and shaky, her gloved hands quivering, her breathing somewhat erratic. She kept her face away from Maria the whole time she'd been back, and certainly refused to look at her after she had stormed out of the V-wing. She was pissed. There was still some unloading to do and Maria had not done it.

Anya stood by the rover, leaned on hand against it as if trying to relocate her anger into the vehicle somehow. "You coming?" she finally asked.

Maria's own fury was high yet contained behind her chest. Her breath was tight. "I'll walk," she replied. "I have my torch."

"The habitat's that way," Anya pointed, moving around to the driver's side. "Tower spotlight is on, so you can't miss it."

"Right."

Anya stopped for a moment and seemed to waver on her feet. "If you feel so inclined you can bring the last of the supplies. Just remove the forward hatch and use it as a sled."

Then without saying another word she strapped the boxes in place, climbed into the rover and drove off into the haze.

* * *

In the next few hours, Maria was taking her time getting to the habitat. She often strayed from the path, searching for more pools and gathering data on what she found along the way. She used the rover's tread marks in the ice to help keep her sense of direction. Behind her, tied to her waist by a thick cord from the landing gear's hydraulics, trailed a make-shift sled of supplies.

As she wandered she kept her data-pad on full scope, recording all she could get. The data-pad's memory unit was almost maxed. She was surprised to find the black pools of sludge were many in number, and that no other probes had reported this find. But they had crashed just north of the equator, in a zone that had showed exceptionally large quantities of packed water ice. The weather patterns were also seen to shift quickly for some reason (maybe thermal venting?). It could be enough to create the conditions necessary for organics to exist.

"It can't be a random pattern," she told Piers. "There must be some stability. Brief periods when conditions become right, and it rains organic compounds from the upper atmosphere. Hell between that water ice and these compounds there is certainly plenty of the right ingredients."

It sounds reasonable, he replied. *But they'd need heat and liquid water. Water is a necessary solvent to carry on the chemistry for basic lifeforms to evolve.*

In grid-space before her, she studied the information from the many basic experiments Piers was conducting. Subjection to radiation, light, heat, and water. Just then something caught her eye.

"Piers," she said. "Scroll back to Program B. *There!* Did you see that?"

Just caught it now.

A granule quivered in the light.

3
Soul Solution

An automated reply finally came from Cassini. Piers had the short range gain up and was just barely able to receive the signal. *Cassini* was on his way. They would slingshot Saturn to increase speed. Best ETA was fifty-two hours, thirty minutes.

Maria had no response from Anya and Piers tried for almost an hour to reach her over the comm-link. *We have to stay,* Maria thought. *When the Inner System gets wind of this, they'll re-schedule their flights. I'm sure of it.*

Her suit comm chimed. "Maria."

"Anya!"she blurted. "Those granules? They're alive! In stasis. There is a very delicate eco-system in balance here. I can't figure it all out yet, but Piers subjected a sample to heat and water and it moved. Unfolded really. Like a flower, Anya. A flower! And you'll never guess what that flower grew into."

"Maria..."

"A fuzzy! Like a cocoon the granules open up and out comes this microscopic, baby fuzzy which grows at a highly accelerated rate. In this fuzzy stage they are carried on the wind currents and feed off the hydrocarbons."

"Maria would you stop for a moment."

"They need heat and water to transform from granule to fuzzy. Heat and water. Anya, the crash. When we hit the heat from our engines melted the surrounding ice pack. Enough for a hatching. That's why we saw them floating *up* from around us. Not *by* us."

"Will you shut up!" Anya said, panic lurked behind the surface of her voice. "I know you're right. The granules are alive."

Maria suddenly sensed Anya's panic. "Are you okay?" she asked.

"Do I sound okay? Shit. I've been in and out of my suit, Maria. And so have you. To change your filter." She paused to breath. "Maria, I'm sick."

Maria glanced down, her light shone on her dirty boots. It didn't take her long to figure it out. "Oh, my God," she whispered. "Anya back when we left the ship, you landed in something. Methane sludge, you said. Are your boots stained?"

"Yes."

She squeezed her eyes shut. Heat filled her ears.

"Anya," she said. "What you thought was methane sludge was Tholin. The damn shit is all over the place. You must have tracked it into the habitat before we knew what it was."

"And you into the Hole."

Maria's pulse quickened.

"It's been examined by the habitat's med-bots. It's small enough to be carried on air, like an aerobic virus. Must propagate quickly in an oxygen-nitrogen atmosphere."

"Anya," Maria's voice was low. "One of the tests showed that under oxy-nitro conditions the granules tend to mutate. Rather violently."

"I've done the med-scan," Anya snapped. "Body's immune system can't cope. It's like a vicious allergic reaction. And it gets worse. This *thing* appears to feed off the body, like a parasite."

Maria felt her body shiver slightly, but she couldn't tell if it was a parasitic infection or simple fear. She felt flush all over. "The body's heat keeps it alive and it draws the necessary nutrients from the blood," she said, as if reading from a textbook. "Oh, Anya..."

"Funny, I've never known a parasite to kill its host. Maria, I'm dying, being eaten alive from the inside. Maria, you have to warn off *Cassini*. Tell Piers...They don't have the abilities to deal with something like this. We didn't. No one has..." her voice broke off.

"Anya!" Maria could smell her own sweat, mixed with the stink of fear.

"Send that message, Maria. Warn them off."

Maria bit her lip and linked with Piers. He sent all the information they had on the contagion. "It's done," she said, weakly.

"Good. Now look. I'm in pain. You will be soon. Horrifying pain. Slow, drawn out..."

Maria conversed with Piers in the link, and while Anya pleaded for her attention they'd decided on what to do.

* * *

Cassini's proximity beacon was moving farther away. They had changed course and were heading back with the news. Although they had been close enough for Piers to download the programs he would need. Some of the medical equipment could be modified, and Anya's geo-tools might just suffice.

There were procedures to follow and Titan would be quarantined, fenced-in, left untouched. The price of failure at Mars, for the death of a fragile eco-system, would be that any plausible candidates for life would have immediate protection until such life could be studied under controlled conditions without risk to either side.

Anya Pushkin had completely succumbed less than an hour later. In her last moments she had spent most of her time vomiting her decaying insides out, and babbling. Finally she had been reduced to a semi-catatonic state, curled up in the fetal position, shaking violently.

Maria, unable to watch her suffer any longer, managed to drag her out of the habitat. Cradling her head in her arms she cried.

Shit! Shit! Okay. Okay. Ready? Do it!

Choking back her fear for only a moment, Anya's helmet latches undone, she twisted the bubble off and let Anya drop to the ice. There came a gagging sound, muffled and distant through her own helmet. The sound of Anya Pushkin dying. Maria turned her back, the acid of her own bile rising in her throat. She wished her helmet was sound proof.

Maria dropped to her knees, hugging her stomach and rocking herself back and forth. *This has to work. God, please let it work!*

There was no way of knowing what the effects would be on her psyche should she go through the entire process while still alive. The procedure of nano-transference was done only after the patient had expired, and in the interest of preserving her memories and cognitive abilities as best they could that was exactly what she had to do: expire, to die, if only for a brief moment.

The nanos would then spread out en-mass, jolting the specified areas of brain tissue with electric surges to reanimate them just enough to remove and record what was needed. And after the nanos had collected and uplinked her memories from her still uninfected mind and into Pier's spare organic casing, she would be alive.

And eventually they would come back. Not *Cassini* but some other ship. Eventually. And she would be waiting.

Am I like this tiny granule? she thought. *Changing form, adapting, acquiring a new function...*

An ocean of possibilities swam before her, licked at her mental heels with each new wave of thought and speculation. The fuzzies, the underground ocean, the hydrocarbons, the Tholin pools of black death, of life, all teetered in her mind's eye.

Maria Osbourne was still kneeling in the slush and ice. Dancing around her were the rolling clouds of hydrocarbons, moving sinuously, changing form. The patter of ethane rain sounded against her faceplate. Nearby, the med-bots waited...

She undid the first latch on her helmet. A red warning light came on.

This is it, she thought. *So will I be reborn? Renewed? Will I know of my life, my whole existence? Will I know who I truly am? Will I know...*

The questions raced at her as the freezing death crept by, a specter that would soon work through every membrane, every cell, stopping blood, freezing thought.

She pulled at the second latch. Her emergency siren began to scream.

And will I be me? All of me? Life, heart, soul, living again?

She felt a strange calmness unknown to her before, working through her body.

Life is defined by what it does. Isn't it?

She undid the last latch and without thinking any further she pulled off her helmet, let it fall to the ground, and with arms outstretched she felt what no one had ever felt before: ethane rain on her face. As the haze of Titan fell away the deathly, freezing cold gave way to a new and pleasant numbness.

It is done.

And in those few seconds before the pressures ripped at her flesh, before the blood filled her ears, rushed from her exploding capillaries to crystallize on her skin, before unconsciousness overtook her, she knew, in those last moments, that she would remember it all.

BOXBOY

I live in a box. A big, big box. It's just white all around, all the walls, even the floor and ceiling. There's no windows. Very boring. No colors. I sit here most of the time and play with my toys. That's the only really neat part. I get lots of toys. Yeah. I like that. And I sit in the center of the big box-room all of the time. That's where they put me, where the doctors want me to be, in the center of the room in my own little box. A box inside a box. I think I saw something like that once with wooden dolls. Open a doll and there's another one inside, and another inside that, and another inside that. They call them Babushka dolls, I think the Woman Doctor told me. Babushka. Well, that's me; I'm a boy in a box surrounded by another box where the doctors are and–so they tell me–inside and even bigger box they call a building. That's a lot of boxes.

I didn't always live in a box, but I couldn't live on the outside anymore. That's what they told me. My body was dying and so they put me in a box so they could continue studying my Talents. There was something strange about my body, it didn't look right, like other peoples, and that's why my Mommy left me. She was very upset. I can just remember. She was always sick, too. Then she finally went to Heaven, where I'm sure she's happier. Daddy left a long time ago, and mommy said something about him not being good at handling the strain. They fought a lot. Mommy was very angry. I hate him for making her angry. He was a bad man. But anyway, they put me here and told me that one day I'll get to walk on the outside again in some kinda new body, and that I just needed to play along with them and their games for a while. Okay?

I like games.

Yeah.

* * *

I'm very talented.

That's what they tell me, anyway. But I don't see anything talented about moving things around the room. I guess they just like the way I do it, the way I play with them. There's a Woman Doctor, Kandis, who's really neat. She plays with me all the time. She like to play as much as I do, and that's a lot. I run my small electric trucks around the room, do little things for her with them, like picks things up and what not.

She's sitting on the floor, cross-legged like Mommy did, and has a controller in her hand for her truck. I don't need one; that's why I'm talented; I move mine from inside my box. They plug a cable into the back of my box, and that's how I do it. I don't quite understand, it has something to do with an...amp...amp...li..fi..fica..fication unit, she calls it. Or something.

When I'n done doing her little things for her, we race our trucks around and around the room. It's great fun; I almost always win. Sometimes we crash them into each other. She says "Ooops!" and laughs. (We're not suppose to do that, ya know, play rough with the toys. Shhh!)

She's the fun one. Most definitely. There's this other Doctor, a man, Dorian, but he's so gloomy. He gets kinda funny when we have too much fun. He's a poo-poo head.

She gets up and says it's time for her to leave now, and that she's very sorry. I say it's okay, because I know I'll see her again at the same time tomorrow. Then she unhooks the cable from my box and puts it on the floor. Sometimes, before she does that, she does something called a "reroute" to an outside camera and I get to see outside. Wow! I'd love to see outside again, the big trees, all green, and that big sky so far up there I could never touch it but always like to think I can if I climb one of those big trees. I ask her about it. I'd really like to see it again, please, please, please, *pleeeeeease!* But this time, she shakes her head. Later.

Rats.

I wish I had a new body, then I could climb those trees and touch the sky, maybe paint some clouds on it, like God does.

I ask her, "When are you gonna let me outta here?"

She doesn't answer. Her face looks funny for a minute, like she bit into a lemon or something. Then she smiles. I get that nice feeling inside.

I like it when she smiles.

* * *

I get to play with the big trucks!

The Woman Doctor brought in a bunch of new trucks to play with. *Big* ones. She said I could play with them for a while. Doctor Dorian starts arguing with her about something, about this being all too soon for me, but I think she won, as she turns to me and winks in one of my many eyes. I call him Doctor Doom because he always has a big sourpuss on his face. She laughs and pets my box. He turns around and leaves for the Doctor Box.

"Okay," she says. "Let's enjoy ourselves!"

Sounds good to me.

"Let's see how well you can play with these." She connects a wire to my box. I feel a slight jolt as she pushes it in. It doesn't hurt, but my vision blurs for a moment. There's a slight crackle...There I can see again, and I'm inside the truck, or I can see out of its eyes. Whatever. Something like that, anyway. This is my first time inside a real truck. Usually they just let me play with them from my box. But this is something new, she says, something that will make me able to be inside a truck. Yeah. Inside a truck, driving it instead of playing with it from my box.

I tell her the trucks eyes are clouding over. She does something, touches something on a metal board and my vision comes back.

"How's that?" she asks me. I tell her fine. I can move the wheels and turn the truck around in circles.

This is great! Yeah! Varoom! Varoom! I'm a truck!

I stop and I see my box, the one I'm suppose to be in. I can see inside it, all the pink water and wires coming out of me. That grey thing with the long tail. That's me. For a moment I feel weird, looking at myself, looking at myself like *that*. I don't understand, but I feel...really strange. Anyway, they said I'll be able to walk again in a new body. Someday. "Soon," she used to say. "Soon." But I've been here a long time. So long, long, long...

I like being a truck, too. The Woman Doctor lets me do what I feel like, for the most part, and I have lots of fun. This truck has six arms, and I use them to pick up things, like chairs and big rocks they bring in to me. Then it gets harder: They bring in a big slice of a valley and ask me to climb to the other side. I get stuck at the bottom. I push my wheels but they just spin. I'm stuck on a rock.

"Think now," she says. "What can you do?"

I think. I push down on the big rock with two of my arms and my front wheels touch the top of the rock. "That's it!" she says. "That's it!" And I push and push and I drive over the boulder and make it to the other side. I drive up the rocky hill to the top, pushing stones out of my way with my arms. In a weird way I feel alive, like I have a new body, like the truck is my new body. But a better one, a stronger one than before.

"Yes!" she screams and claps her hands. I stop at the top of the hill and look down at her. She's smiling and says something to the ceiling. I hear Doctor Doom reply, "Let's not be premature, Kandis." I don't like his voice. He can be mean.

"Augh, really!"

He doesn't like it when we get "so close" he says. He says "its not good for you, it's not good for him, blah, blah, blah..." Daddy said something like that once, that Mommy and I were "to attached" at the hip. Whatever that means. I didn't even have hips.

I flash the lights of the truck at her. She laughs. I reach out, through darkness, and move the big metal arm in one corner of the room. I reach out and she puts her hand out. I shake hands with her. She looks surprised. I like to surprise her.

"What else can you do at once?"

The smaller trucks in the room begin to whirr. I make them run around the room and stop at her feet. "Oh, my!" she says. "That was very good. I didn't know you could move more than one thing at a time. How long have you been able to do that?"

I dunno.

She steps over the trucks, comes to the bottom of the hill and smiles up at me, just like Mommy when she used to hold me over her head. "You're so very talented, Adam,"she says. "Very, very talented."

Yeah.

"How would you like to drive one or two of these trucks on Pluto?" she asks. "That's another world *very* far away in space. Hum?"

Yeah! Really? Neat!
Varoom!

* * *

I hurt today.

They're doing something to me, something called "modifications". It hurts! Owe! It *hurts!* The Woman Doctor says I'll get better soon, and she's so very worried that I hurt so much. "There, there," she says. "I'm here, Adam. I'm here." *Make it stop!* "Very soon, love. Very soon. Hang in there, okay?" I can't see clearly. Everything is fading in and out. The pain, it's like those headaches I use to get before. Dorian argues with the Woman Doctor about something they're doing.

"He had the capability to reach beyond his present abilities."

"But that type of power?" she says. "It could overload him. The tests aren't *that* conclusive. I think you're going too far."

"Nonsense. He's ready for this."

She's getting angry.

Stop it! You're a bad man!

He looks into my eyes. "Stay out of this!"

"Don't talk to him like that!"

They argue for a while longer. The pain is getting worse. I wish they'd stop the pain. And I don't like it when they yell so much.

Mommy!

"Now look what you've done," she says. "You've upset him."

"Take a break, Kandis."

She leaves the room in a huff, stomping her feet.

"Well," says Doctor Doom. "Don't you worry about her. Let's see what we can do about finishing this job." He does something and the pain is fading away. Gone. There's a truck outside somewhere. He wants me to try and reach out to it, to move it around if I can. I feel for it, the truck. Feel around, like when I'm in the dark after they turn my eyes off at night. After a while I find it, can see out of its eyes. Wow! Everything is so green, and the sky is a wonderful blue, and the sun so yellow. I can see birds. There are birds up there in the sky! They're just like I remember them. And the trees are so big. Yeah, maybe I'll get to climb one of those trees someday, in my new body. I wish, I wish, I wish. I never got to do it before, either. But I wasn't right then.

"There," says Doctor Doom, and plugs something into me. "All ready."

I feel something strange, now, like a feeling of...of being big. *Real* big! Like I could do almost anything, see anything, like I could reach out, touch everything, be *everywhere!*

"Beautiful, isn't it?" asks the Woman Doctor from the Doctor Box. I agree. "Just think of all the beautiful places you could go like this. You can go anywhere on Earth, in space. To see the beauty of space. Wouldn't that be exciting? Isn't this such a great game?"

Oh, yes! Yes, yes, yes!

She giggles.

Could I get a real body, too?

Maybe.

I love you!

                  * * *

"Stop that!" he yells at me.

I'm playing with my smaller trucks, running them around the room, past his legs, under a table stacked with some machines. He's trying to work, or something. Doctor Doom. I ask him why.

"Because I said so!" he barks at me. Even I know that's no answer. I keep playing with my truck because I am bored. I get bored a lot when I am not playing with the Woman Doctor.

I bump his leg.

"Will you stop it!"

No! The Woman Doctor says I don't have to worry about you.

"Kandis!"

She comes inside from the Doctor Box. "What is it, now?" They argue again. "Let him have some fun, will you?" He starts to talk loudly. She does too. They start yelling and yelling and yelling. "You're too close, too emotionally involved, Kandis. Good God!" She screams back at him.

Stop it! Stop it! Stop it!

"You are not the head of this project!" he yells and pushes a finger in her chest. She stumbles back.

Hey, don't you touch her!

"Neither are you, Doctor Doom!"

"Very funny! But I'd seriously think about my approach if I were you. All sweet, promises, promises, acting like he was your own kid. Look, I'm sorry your kid died, but–"

"You're way out of line, Doctor." They go on and on. No one is listening to me. I'm getting angry. Angry at him. I move the bigger truck from the corner of the room.

"I'm gonna suggest you take some leave."

"Take some yourself!"

You leave her alone! I drive up to him and grab his leg with one of my arms. I hear something crack and he yells. *Stop it! Stop it! You leave her alone!* I push him away from her and he falls to the floor, holding his leg.

"Adam!"

You're a bad man! A very bad man! I hate you!

"Get that thing away from me!" he shouts, trying to get up.

I feel strange again. I push outward into darkness. I feel...I feel...Suddenly I can see everything. Everything! I'm looking through thousands of eyes, everywhere. I can see all the other boxes, all the busy people. I can even see outside.

He tries to move toward the door. I lock it on him. I lock all the doors, everywhere. The computer speaks: "Security Activated."

"Adam, what are you doing?" she asks.

I hit him, like I use to hit Daddy when he made Mommy upset. *Bad! Bad! Bad man!*

"Adam, stop!" But I don't. I hate him! I hate him! He makes her so upset. I want him to stop. To stop forever. She's crying. She's crying. I must make him stop!

"Adam!"

I blow out the light bulbs in most of the big box. It rains bits of fire.

I hit him once more and he stops. He doesn't move anymore.

"Adam!" She's at the table of machines. She's getting quiet. I think she's happier, now. We'll both have more fun. She won't have to go on leave, whatever that is. She can give me a new body, and play with me outside, and hold me up over her head, just like Mommy.

She sits all quiet like in the chair. She looks a little scared. Look what he did to her. He was a very bad man.

"Oh, Adam." She's playing with one of the machines.

What a bad man. Bad.

She doesn't answer. I can see from my truck's eyes, and the blue water starts to come into my box's water. What's that?

Hey. We can have all the fun we want. I wanna go to Pluto. How far away is Pluto?

She isn't listening. Something's happening. I feel sleepy. Very sleepy. This is weird, I'm never tired inside my box.

I can get my new body, right? We can play with our trucks, and I can climb the trees and paint some clouds on the sky. When's it gonna happen? Huh? When?

She's crying again. I don't know why.

Why are you crying? Why am I so tired?

She's not listening, and there's one thing I'd like to ask her, again.

When are you gonna let me outta here?

MEMORY WITHOUT PAIN

The sun burns in the sky and makes my eyes hurt.

I wander through the crowded streets of Chayne to the place where we had agreed to meet. It's a shabby old tavern on the corner of two deadbeat walkways; dust and trash blow in the streets like tiny animals. Other low castes push their way through the alleys or sit in filthy doorways or lean out of broken windows. Some stare at me and I don't like it. I feel uncomfortable, as if they can see what I really am. I pull my jacket around me, tight, as if I can really hide behind it but feeling better all the same. A wind blows past me, temporarily relieving the heat of day. I see my destination and I make my way through the stone arches and down into the damp dark of the tavern. I find him in the far corner of the bar, pulling at an ale.

Bastard.

He nods. "You look well, Fenn."

I nod back and take a seat. He has dressed down, more casual, more normal like the rest of us. "As well as I can be, Arat," I reply, looking over many heads and out the front window at the low caste children, scavenging through a rubbish bin, cloths smeared with filth.

"How's Myra?" he says mechanically. "Still fighting?"

"As usual," I reply.

"Strong headed woman, that one," he says strangely. "I don't know if I should consider you lucky or not."

"Right," I say. I hate this small talk but I go along with it each time I meet with him. As if he really cares about what the hell is going on in my life. I continue to act submissive, remembering the bruises on my left rib cage and rubbing my fingers over them. My dreams of Myra, Myra falling, return briefly. A puff of smoke.

He orders me an ale and when delivered I pull at it long and hard. He takes out a small disk and throws it across the table at me, information for my next job. It contains yet another name from a long list of names of people I don't know. It also contains a small needle of the kill-drug Primal-44, to inject into my neck before the job. I am an assassin by trade.

"Not the usual pace to arrange my next assignment," I say, pocketing the disk and eyeing him suspiciously. I wish he'd just be forward for once. I hate this, I really do.

"Things change," he says, throwing me another little disk. My special little stash of brain candy. "I had to see you immediately, inconspicuously, to deliver some good news, and some bad. We've a totally new technique. I thought you might be interested in it."

"In what?" I ask, fingering the disk of drugs, longingly. I really need a smack of bliss. I've been out for some time.

He ducks his head and takes a sip of his ale. "We have a breakthrough."

"Not interested," I blurt out, catching on. "And there's nothing in my contract that states you can force me." I had heard this story more than once, and each person who tried it had lost everything, every memory of every person and place and idea that ever existed for them. Complete memory detonation. It was a clean wipe that either stripped out bits of one's life or reduced a person down to a suckling infantile idiot.

I want the bloody nightmares gone, and badly, but let them come up with a proven method first. Until then I would rather go slowly mad, or blow my brains out altogether.

Arat Idriss shakes his head. Funny, he doesn't appear to be sweating like me. He looks cool, like the heat is passing around him.

"I know what happened to those who tried the treatment,"

I say, feeling the heat of rage building up. Sweat runs down my temples.

"No, no," he says. "We've reversed the process, leaving in the undesired memory but *cutting off* the emotional response to that particular memory."

That catches me off guard.

"That's right," he says, smiling.

I don't reply.

His eyes glow. "Yes," he says. "A neural cap. Null response. This will increase the proficiency of our employees. *Your* proficiency!"

I sit in silence for a moment and think about what he has just said. *Memory without pain?* As if they would make everything okay.

That Primal-44 is a drug which, when injected into the recipient, activates the most aggressive urges to kill. All the savage, angry feelings brought to the surface in a concentrated ball of fury. A rage-magnifier, I call it. An assassin's best friend, especially since weapons could not make it past the inner city's sensors. The Prime is undetectable, and you never know who's doped up until it's too late.

Activated by visual stimulation (a target has been identified) there is no way to stop it, and the recipient must act out the aggression to its bloody conclusion. And I remember every gruelling second, every broken neck, every shattered head, every ripped torso, everything. Those few who are able to use the prime are "drafted" into service. I am one of the lucky few.

My face must display my doubts about the treatment, as Arat quickly adds: "Okay, it's not foolproof, I'll admit it. It could rid you of some other emotions to particular memories, but at least it will rid you of your shakes, your nausea, your..."

"Conscience" I add, sourly.

He sits back in his chair and gives me the once over, somewhat amused by my tone of voice. "Conscience is but a weakness, Fenn. A weakness which has no place here, let alone in the minds of our employees. It cripples ambition."

"Your ambition. And I piss on your solution," I reply. "From complete memory erasure to emotional desensitization. So what's the bad news?"

He seems to stare right through me for a moment. This time he doesn't look amused. "We think something is going down. A few of our other agents have failed to report in; we found three the other day, but you wouldn't want to know the condition we found them in. We think word of this new drug has been leaked to someone on the outside, which could account for the increase in activity these past few weeks. What's in it for the leak, you ask? Who knows. Money. A pardon for a relative. The dissolution of a contract. And the other Houses are beginning to grumble again. But then when did they ever really stop." His lip curls.

I watch him. It always seems like a game to him, doesn't it?

"As far as your shadow is concerned, we're still running background checks on a few individuals. We have some leads. We'll find him."

"I hope to God you do!" I say. "Do you know what it's like walking around, always having to look over your shoulder? You said it was almost impossible for anyone to find out our identities. Even the identities of other employees."

"Almost" he reiterates. "As with everything nothing is foolproof, I suppose. What we have here is a very clever, and dangerously curious, individual."

I look around nervously at the many faces across the bar.

"No one here," he says, casually dismissing the loud and lewd crowd of commoners. "No one gives a damn what we're talking about. You know that. And besides," he says, pulling out a small device from his pocket, "I always use my scrambler when I meet someone like this. Our conversations are safe."

I start to breath faster. The stiff air is hard to suck into my lungs. I feel as if I'm going to suffocate.

"The funny thing is," he says, leaning forward, "is that these problems began when your shadow appeared."

"I don't know how much more I can take," I say quickly.

He shakes his head. "Sorry."

"But you said maybe...well...maybe I could..."

"Did I?" he replies, coldly. "You knew what you were getting yourself into."

As if I had a choice!

"There's a little killer in everyone, Fenn. Don't you think?"

I down the rest of my ale and throw a few coins at him across the table. He scoffs and leaves the coins where they fell. "If you'll excuse me," I say, about to get up. "I have better things to do with my time."

A smile slithers its way across his dark face. "You forget yourself, Fenn. You forget who you work for. You need this procedure. You're getting sloppy. Someone almost found you last time. I won't stand for mistakes of this magnitude."

"What are you going to do? Kill me?"

"Now what purpose would that serve?"

I try to get up. He leans across the table and grabs my arm. "Fenn, you're still our best. My best. The savagery you have deep inside yourself. I don't want to find you dead somewhere. I can't afford it. The procedure can give you at least part of what you want: Escape. That's what you want, isn't it?"

I whip my arm free and stand up, amazed at my courage for a moment. I want to escape, yes. But not the kind he is offering. I'll stick to bliss, thank you.

"My best pupil," he says. "Brutal and savage and with a stomach like jelly."

I want to give him my best "piss off" look but instead I look ashamedly at the floor, like a good little servant.

"You'll call me," he adds, confidently. "Sooner or later." He throws another disk of bliss at me, grinning his stupid little grin.

I pick it up, knowing I'm going to need it, turn around and head for the door. As I push my way out I hear his voice over the bar noise. "I'll expect your call, Fenn!"

I almost slam the door.

* * *

I want out. I need out. I hate this whole thing. This place.

Arat. Fleeting images of dreams, lost yearnings flash through my mind. Hopes long gone after Arat had taken my life away. Her life. I get angry. The heat of the endless Preen summer doesn't help my disposition.

I stare down at my bloody hands, hands that had killed and would continue to kill. How many lives have I destroyed? How many necks have I broken, bodies have I broken, with these hands? I sit and curse my ugly, shaking hands.

As I slowly start to come down off the Prime I notice a body near me. I don't want to look but I do, and throw up. My stomach twists. Blood. Too much blood. I get up and the room spins. I steady myself. "Bastard!" I hear myself say. I reach into my pocket and take out the disk, pop it open, and gulp down a pill of bliss. I want it to work fast. I stumble out and into the street, crashing through a sluice filled with stagnant water.

I go to a public receiver and call home. Myra doesn't answer. I sit on the pavement and wonder where she could be now. Does it really matter? Do I really want to know?

I sit and let my mind spin.

"Bastard!" I say again. I think about losing her. I always think about losing her, next to all the blood. She is the only beautiful thing I have in this world. A model of perfection untouched by the chaos of living in this nation-state.

I know I must check in with Arat to confirm the hit, but all I want to do is go home, hold her in my arms and cry. My stomach churns a bit more.

After a moment I get up and set out into the darkness I wish I could call my friend.

* * *

I stumble into my apartment at about two in the morning, as sick as one can be. The floor keeps swaying to and fro as if I were on the deck of a ship on rough waters. My limbs are shaking and I feel like I could vomit yet again.

I had run a steel pike, God knows how many times, into some poor bastard's head.

I slam up against a wall and slide down it halfway. I try to hold in a cry, my stomach turns, bile rises in my throat. Nice drug, that Primal-44.

From the corner of the dark room someone moves in the bed. "Fenn, you woke me up!" The voice is sleepy, yet wonderfully, wonderfully warm. It pulls me up out of the pit of my stomach. I push myself up off the wall and steady myself.

"Sorry, Myra," I say, and try to make my way over to the bed.

"No you don't!" she snaps, raising herself on one arm. "You go wash yourself off and burn those cloths before you even *think* about getting into bed."

I look down to see my shirt and hands are stained with blood, bits of grey matter slosh in my breast pocket. Fluid rushes in my throat and I barely make it to the bathroom in time. The sour taste of bile fills my mouth and spills out; its stench stains the air.

I strip off my sweat and blood soaked garments, turn on the shower and step under the warm water. I stand there for a moment under the falling water, gathering much needed strength, washing the stench and filth of life away. It's a slice of heaven to feel clean for the moment.

The flashes return, hover before my eyes in violent light. "Go away!" I say into my now shaking hands.

"What?" Myra's voice comes from the other room.

"Nothing," I reply. "Nothing at all." I step out to the sink again, pull the disk out of my jacket pocket and open it. Six wonderful white pills lay there, waiting for me. I finger one and hold to it like it is my savior. My heart is racing in my chest and I look at myself in the dirty mirror. So it's come to this, has it? To this, to this, to this. I swallow the pill and wait for the first tingle of bliss to take effect again.

I dry myself off and shuffle back into the bedroom.

"Who were you talking too?"

"Myself, Myra," I say. "Myself."

"What again?" she says flatly. "When are you going to quit living like this? Look what's happened to you!" She sighs and buries her face in her pillow. "Fenn," she continues. "You can't keep doing this. You know that. I can't live every day worrying about you."

"Don't start with me," I warn her, sitting on the edge of the bed.

I hear her turn over and she speaks to my back: "Oh, you can't be careful all the time. Why don't we just run away? Somewhere. Anywhere! Remember when we were kids..."

She worries so much about me, that I'll be next on someone's list, that I won't come home. I can almost feel the tears welling up in her eyes, her throat tightens.

You still are a kid, my love. But just barely. And it's been hard enough keeping you away from all this. How long do you have? How long?

"Myra, it's not that easy," I reply. She has never met or seen Arat. She is not suppose too. She has no idea how difficult this whole thing can be.

"We could go to Polis, up north," she says. "They're a neutral state. Or we could find transport to one of the offworld colonies. I know this guy who can.....What?"

"Myra, you're not listening."

"Oh, I've heard it all before," she snorts and rolls back over, her long dark hair swishes past my face. A scent of fresh blossoms. "Why won't you let me help?"

She's falling, I remember. Falling away from me in my dreams. I reach for her, grab her hand, but she slips into darkness.

"You know I....uh...Myra."

"Don't say another word!"

I reach over and touch her. "Myra."

She wriggles away from my hand. "Don't touch me!"

I pull my hand back, heavily. I want to reach out to her, to tell her everything will be fine. But we both know that is a lie, and I have hurt her enough without resorting to telling her lies.

"I called earlier," I say. "Where were you?"

The sheets rustle. "In town," she says, meekly.

"What were you doing out so late?"

She doesn't reply at first. "I was at Helena's"

"Oh," I reply, not very convincingly. "That's in Green District, isn't it?"

Silence. A sigh. "That's right."

"That's a few blocks from where I was, isn't it?"

She lies under the sheets, barely breathing. "How am I suppose to know where you go?"

"Yeah."

I think about the money I've saved up, in case I ever decided to run away with her. It seems like the only way, as I am losing her more and more as each day passes. However, I know, deep down inside, that they would find us eventually. Arat and his men. No low caste leaves a contract. I think she knows that too, but it's the small chance of hope that fills her heart. With no thanks to me, hope is the only thing she has left to cling too.

* * *

I wake up to find Myra gone. I am disappointed by not very surprised.

I eat breakfast and shuffle out the door and into the burning daylight. My pores release their salty fluids that run over me. I am soaked before I even make it down the length of the street.

Nothing to do now but wait.

I keep walking.

Wait for the next pick up today.

I keep walking.

For some reason blistered into the back of my mind, I decide to make *him* wait.

* * *

I can't sleep tonight.

I walk the dark streets alone with my thoughts, long coat over my shoulders to fight off the damp night chill. Sewer water runs in a nearby gutter. I listen to its soft rhythm as it runs its way through the night. Then I hear something. A sound almost buried by the trickling water. I think I'm being followed. My heart almost bursts in my chest; I pick up my pace. It still seems to be getting closer. It's that shadow, isn't it? How long has he been following me? And who are you? Who? My mind blossoms fear, and it doesn't help that I'm high on bliss, either.

I take a side alley and almost break into a run. Did he see me? I think I hear something, footsteps, maybe. I continue my little game of ducking down side alleys. I think I lost him, and for a moment, thinking about that, I feel slightly disappointed...

I walk for an hour, as the bliss trickles down to nothing. Reality begins to return in its cruel entirety; the night seems darker, the filth that much more apparent, the decay and stench of the city fills my nostrils. Groups of people, haggard and warn and probably as high as the moons, sit in various corners of alleys and under dark awnings, chattering to themselves or simply staring out into space.

It begins to rain.

"Hey, I know you!" someone says. I suck in air in fright and look over my shoulder. A man named Piet swaggers in an open doorway. I relax a bit. I used to work with him, scavenging the rubbish dumps outside the city for spare parts to sell. He looks terrible ands smells strongly of urine, even from a few footsteps away.

"Hey, Fenn, man. Could you spare some sweet smoke? For a friend?"

I shake my head sympathetically. "Sorry, I don't have any."

"Some bliss?"

"Not on me," I say, which is a lie. I begin to move on. Better to move on.

"Some money?" he begs. "Hey! How about it? C'mon, man!"

I wave my hand over my shoulder.

"Where you been working?" he calls after me. "Don't see you around much. Hey, Fenn, I heard you dope up the Prime."

I stop and turn around. I feel nothing for a moment. My mind is blurry. "I don't know where you get your information from, Piet. I'd be very careful about rumors if I were you. They get people hurt." I try to be as natural as possible, but his comment struck me hard. No one on the outside is suppose to know who works for the Houses, and this sort of thing getting around can really make your day. Especially when another faction goes looking to bump off employees. That kind of information can go for a very good price if anyone got the nerve to try and sell it, what with reciprocation being what it is. But then again I've got nobody who'd reciprocate. I only have Myra. Myra.

But all it takes is one desperate fool.

"Tsk, tsk," he slurs at me. Obviously been drinking lamp spirits. "Why so touchy? Too close to the truth for your liking, *assassin?*"

People begin looking at me. I feel the air tighten. Voices mumble around me. The rain seems to be coming down faster, harder, running down my face. I walk over to him.

"Piet," I calmly rage, in a controlled voice only he can hear. "Think carefully about what you say. The House doesn't think rumors are very...socially acceptable. And they think losing things that might be of value equally unacceptable. What do you value?" I look over at his wife and daughter in the doorway. "Think carefully about what you say, and to whom!"

He straightens up a bit, trying to push his chest out. He looks like he is going to say something, then relents, his face dropping and he closes the door. The onlookers slowly turn back to their business. I turn back around and keep walking.

I don't know why I breath a sigh of relief, or said what I did, as I secretly hope to get caught out, anyway. I know that. I only hope it will be quick and painless. However a part of me, for some reason beyond imagining, wins out against such an idea. I guess my animal instinct for survival is alive and well after all.

* * *

Tonight I ride the shuttle bus around and around through the night, waiting. I must have passed my stop a dozen times or more.

And out there, somewhere, some poor bastard doesn't know what's coming...

I watch the dark cityscape go by again and again, thinking of how much I hate Arat Idriss. Like a cancer he spreads his dark arms out over the city, over me, holding us all, holding us, smothering us...I feel myself beginning to boil like water. I suddenly realize I'm banging my head against the window.

Myra. My dreams of her falling away down a dark expanse of tunnel become frighteningly real. I must admit I live for her. She is the only thread of sanity left for me to cling too. There is nothing else.

This is going to be my last hit. I've decided. This is it. Damn him to hell this is it! I will tell Myra. We will plan an escape. Maybe Polis, maybe some other world, I don't care anymore. I can't lose her. I am not a killer.

The pain of a hundred or more targets flushes through my stomach. I grip the seat railing and close my eyes. I hear the hum of the engine and somehow it calms me. My stop comes up and I get off. The humidity in the air is like syrup.

I walk along a dark alley and stop under an awning. I look around but there is no one that I can see. I take out the small needle and jab it into my neck. My muscles flinch. I lean back against the stone building, feeling jittery, my blood picking up pace.

This is it. The last one. The last. No more. If it weren't for the incoming fear of what I am about to do next, I could almost feel a sense of relief. I brush my hair back with sweaty hands and sigh heavily.

I make my way through the winding alleys to a place just near Green District and Ankor District. I use my electronic pick to unlock the door. The alarm system has been cut off for me at the main grid. It is dark, and no one is here. Not yet. He won't come for another hour.

I sit in a chair, in the dark, and wait...

* * *

I am in a charm house, doped up pretty good. You pay a small entrance fee and get a bed, some food, and you can even buy some stuff if you happen to be dry. A very decent set up, and after such a shit night I need a place like this badly (I keep seeing that poor bastard's smashed head). The heavenly tingle running through my body is better than sex, always that final rushing before the end, but never quite reaching it. I hug my arms around my waist and wish it could last forever.

Smoke floats around the room like the long tails of desert lizards, creeping and winding through the air. The smoke is sweet in scent, pleasant and welcoming. The dive is dimly lit and many low castes are spread out across the room, indulging in their own private paradises. I sit by a small window, looking up at the stars of the night sky and wondering what Edens could be waiting for me, calling my name; the bliss makes it that much easier to imagine.

Oh, yes, Myra. This is it. I can feel the freedom. I can feel it. You will too.

I look up through my haze and see Arat, staring down at me. He shakes his head and steps out of my vision. "Tsk,tsk." Another man comes into view, but before I can utter a word a fist comes down on me, hard. I crumple to the floor.

"Ready for the new treatment?" asks Arat. "No?"

I struggle for air. Someone else picks me up by my shirt and pulls me outside. He throws me on the ground and kicks me in the back.

"It's a shame," says Arat. " You could leave all this behind you." Another fist in my mouth. "Your bitchy girlie." A kick. "Your dope houses." A jab in the kidneys. "Your gutless stomach." Another fist and my head hits the sidewalk with a thud. Things start to blur. "You're the only one holding out. Everyone else practically begged me for it. Think about it." He gives me a hard kick to the ribs. "And that's for making me wait. I hate waiting."

Blood, my own blood, runs down the stone walkway. I hear footsteps walking away. Someone picks me up and throws me into the back of a transport. I think I feel the cold steel of a needle. "Last one," someone says, laughing.

I wake up and hurt all over. The pain is running through me like fluids. My eyes hurt, but I manage to look around me, slowly. I don't recognize this place at first. As things come into clear focus I see I am in the high caste district. There is a growing light on the eastern horizon. The furnace of the sun. It is just dawn.

Struggling to my feet, I recognize this walkway, cleaned and polished by low caste hands. Everything about them is clean and perfect and neat. Every building a masterwork of architecture, every stone in the road evenly spaced out.

I can make out a door a few meters ahead. I drag myself over to it and push the announcement button. At first things are quiet, then there is the sound of footsteps inside, coming toward the door. I stop and look around and it suddenly hits me: I know this place!

A young woman in a robe answers the door, sleepily, her long hair swooshing about her shoulders. She stops, gasps. Her eyes widen, she tries to speak. "Fenn?"

Arat!

Suddenly I feel heat, rage burning inside me. Lightning flashes of red before my eyes. It is like I step out of myself and watch as I grab her by the throat and squeeze. I lift her up off her feet by her neck, move inside the apartment, and slam her up against a wall several times. Balls of fury explode in the air around me. I am breathing hard, sweating, her choking words running past me like wind.

"Fenn!"

I rage and rage and rage.

* * *

I'm on the floor, face down, a thin howl escaping my lips. Everything is quiet except for me. I howl. I shake. I do this for a very long time.

"What were you doing? What were you doing?"

My eyes roll around in my sockets. I feel like I should vomit, but I can not. I am not even shaking anymore. I just lay face down on the floor sucking in air, tingling all over, electric currents running through my veins. I stare at the artificial wood grains of the floor. So it's come to this, has it? To this, to this, to this!

Bastard!

Without looking, I reach over and stroke her bloody hair. My baby girl. My baby. How? How could you help? Help me? How? My darling, darling sister...

I know Arat is not around. He must be at the Intelligence

Department, waiting for me. I don't need the specially encoded Prime, or the new treatment. I know that now. And it is a calm knowledge, almost without proper emotion. Ideas, visions, feelings vanish. Nothing but rolling wastelands of ice. I feel cold, my breath ice.

I'm at the comm-receiver. I key in the number. A secretary answers the line. I tell her to inform Arat I'll be coming. She says she will tell him. I close the line.

I leave the apartment for Government Avenue. As I walk out of the apartment the harsh sun is over the horizon. Funny, I don't appear to feel the heat, to be sweating. I know I should but I feel cool, very cool.

I stare straight ahead at the distant lights of the main buildings. I walk along in my new, cool skin, feeling even the slightest of breezes against my face. The air is crisp, the heat is gone, and the sun rises on a new season.

Winter has come to Preen.

NEXUS

"Can you see anything?"

Alexei brings the binoculars up to his faceplate and peers out at the foggy beachhead to our right. There is a silence as he tries to pierce through the rolling banks of methane smog which flitter across the thick ocean's surface, the only sounds being the humming of the electric engine and the sloshing of sludge-like water underneath the boat.

"I don't see a thing," he replies in a huff. "Are you sure you saw something?"

"Just keep this position."

Alexei rolls his eyes and turns his back to Chan, then squints his eyes as he looks out and over the water again at the approaching land, as if that would help his vision any. He takes a cloth and wipes condensation from his helmet's faceplate, the tiny ice specs in the fog melt against the slight warmth his pressure suit emits.

"The scanners picked up movement in this area just twenty minutes ago," says Chan from the back of the boat. "And the airspace above is clear of ships."

"The scanners must be developing an imagination," I reply.

"Either that or a sense of humor," says Alexei, tersely. "If there is anything left, any large herds at all, it'd be a miracle. We're chasing ghosts."

I hear Chan sigh with irritation over my helmet speakers.

We had come out from the outpost on a small island in the bay, searching, protecting our newly forming eco-system. The daily job as a Chaser team is to cull the indigenous population to acceptable levels. Mine is to bag at least one specimen from whatever we encounter for some tycoon's private zoo down in Delta City. Brings in a hefty sum. A little extra income never hurt.

I hear the muffled sound of a seismic detonator in the distance, cracking the caldera of some sleeping fire god. The thick waters waver slightly with the shockwave. Not to worry about tidal waves. Most seas are only a few meters deep, and there are no tides to speak of.

"Haven't seen a manoi in a good year," I say to no one in particular, focusing on the vastness of the wild spaces beyond the shore.

"Radio in," says Alexei. "Report a false alarm."

"Right." I reach absently for the transmitter on my suit arm.

Despite Alexei's negative outflow, Chan enthusiasm is still getting the best of him as he continues to check and double check his instruments.

Alexei glances back at Chan, working.

"And get that guy a laxative, will ya?"

* * *

We dock at the quay and await our transfer back to the offices at Bio-Control. Chan paces around nervously, like an expectant father, stopping every so often to look out into the forever-rolling methane clouds above. The cool sun can barely be seen through the dense clouds as an orange blur or a brownish smudge in the sky. Some days it can't be seen at all.

I am just glad to get out of that damned sweat suit; the stink of my own body is getting to me. I need a shower. Alexei stretches his limbs, shakes his mane of dark hair and scratches at his beard.

We sit in a large waiting area, watching the people walk by, getting their transfers or going to the few waterfront shops that had just been re-opened after an extremist bombing only a few weeks ago. Yes, it's starting to happen here, too. New tenants bringing new scars. However, the growing Naturalist opposition party deny supporting extremists.

Uh-huh...

Chaser teams aren't immune, and have been known to get ambushed. When I joined ten years ago, I had been caught out in two such attacks. Half my team had been wiped out by grenades on both occasions. We never saw them coming. We only saw them retreat, disappear into the cool methane mists from which they'd sprung. It was known that extremists members sometimes infiltrated teams, leading them right into ambush. Suicide for the infiltrator, but better than getting captured. And besides, it's a cause. Right? Happens that way. Or so I've been told.

But things have been quiet lately. Rumor had it that was about to change again. Three teams had gone missing in the past two standard weeks.

"Drink, Rohan?" Alexei offers, holding out a canister of what we both knew to be some sort of alcoholic brew he'd concocted. I smile and take the canister, place it to my lips, and ready myself for the sting. It is remarkably decent. I hand it back to Alexei who holds it up to Chan. Chan shakes his pudgy, shaved head. Alexei mumbles something and turns away.

I don't really blame Alexei for his attitude. Sometimes I feel the same way. You get a call, you rush around, expecting to bag a big one, then get disappointed when it turns out to be nothing, an unidentified blip, a small transport, anything but what you *really* want it to be. The damned things have become so elusive lately. Pranks make it worse; they inflame a brief flurry of exuberance that soon fades like the "flimph" of paper on fire.

Damn, I'd like that money!

Chan is new on the job, which counts against him in the annoying department. He's younger than most, and his child-like enthusiasm can make it all rather unbearable at times. Funny enough, he's not out to bag a trophy, like most of us. Like me he's out to capture one. Hell, as many as possible for the planned reservations. Yeah, the government is planning a few, even though this government sponsored project is heading for downsizing, to be added to the non-priority list. Which is not a bad thing, really. Makes more room for private business. More money for me.

"If you don't stop pacing," says Alexei, "I'm gonna break your legs."

Chan glares at him and takes a seat away from us. "Where's that damned transport?" he asks, drumming his fingers on his helmet in his hands and craning his neck to see out the huge bay window.

"An hour from here," I say. "So cool your jets. We'll file a report, go home and drink a lot. Another hard day's work."

I feel sour, thinking about the commission I might lose.

* * *

We spend the time discussing the species of this world, Australius, from the tiny ice moles to the large prey, the ones we hunt, the manoi, air flitters who resemble large manta rays of old Earth, but with wispy tentacles that waver about like Medusa's hair. The creatures were named after Hans Manoi, the man who had unfortunately ran into a herd at Arrival Point to the south of Beta Junction. His landing party were never seen again, but pieces of a body were picked up a few days later, scattered over a kilometer. It took a DNA tag to identify him as Hans.

Alexei does his best to stay out of the conversation and smokes a cancer-free cigarette, lying back against two cushions. Chan speaks about the self-regulating systems of worlds, the Gaia Mothers, the balance out of whack. Although I can't quite understand Chan's philosophies—a fusion of early twenty-first century eco-New Age Gaia worship and Taoism—I can admire his passion. You can see it in his eyes. It may be attributed to his youth, his naive enthusiasm for the "natural order" of things, but it amounted to little more than heated debates or boring speeches we only half listened to.

Being a Naturalist member of the popular sect known as "The Way," Chan had volunteered for this post rather than applied for it. And we certainly hadn't asked for a guy with next to zero qualifications. But the government seems pleased to take on volunteers for government work.

"Artificial eco-systems will never fully stabilize," Chan contests.

"How long do you think we can live on synthetics alone? How long can a controlled climate hold? Learn from history. Whenever a great answer to a great question is found, nature eventually comes along and changes the formula, re-calibrates, fine tunes. Remember what happened at Mars?"

Alexei grumbles, "So someone screwed up. Happens."

Being one of the few Firsts left, I remember the catastrophe well. Re-activating the volcanoes of the Tharsis ridge to speed up the atmosphere project had cracked the once solid Martian plates. Earthquakes shook the New World almost endlessly for an entire decade. And with the old bacteria awakening, and new diseases spreading out like locusts, Mars was uninhabitable for almost a century.

"The forces of Tao," Alexei says, mimicking a deep and reverent voice. "We and the universe are one. Mother Gaia, Father Cosmos. It is all divine. Seek yea, harmony, harmony, *harmony!*"

That did it. I crack up. Chan is straight-faced. I put my hands up, as if fending off an attack that never comes.

"You heard the news reports before you left," he says. "Hell, man, you were there! The increase in weather shifting; the blizzards in the middle of a hot summer day; ocean swells swallowing huge chunks of land. You were there!"

It was all true, but dismissed as flukes in the system that must sometimes occur. We'd terraformed Earth to suit our specific needs, and with the transformation of other system worlds and moons, starvation and unemployment went down to ten percent of the overall population. It was hard to imagine why anyone would want to preserve an eco-system we obviously had no need for anymore. We'd constructed kilometers of architecture that would rival even the stone geniuses of ancient Europe. We'd let people hunt, for food or sport, driving the animals out and into the cities where they took on an aggressive if not ravenous approach to humankind. Some were saved in privately sponsored zoos. Most either died or were eventually destroyed, effectively putting an end to raw meat consumption. Protein was obtained from other sources. Reserved areas of land were used mainly for agriculture, and what was not grown was synthesized. Ironically, after millions of years, we'd become an agricultural society again, the only part of our new lifestyle the extremists agreed with. And it all stemmed from violent eco-shaping technology. It was the easiest way to feed the over two hundred billion people of Homeworld.

Some people blockaded government buildings during the early phases; others tied themselves to trees in forests marked for destruction, or took animals into their homes without permits. Still others did the outrageous and set themselves on fire at the world summits.

What we were doing was our best to alleviate the Great Depression of the twenty-first century, that had plunged most of the world's population into depravity. Our fleets of sleeper ships, migrating outward in droves like an ancient herd of buffalo, were merely an extension of that desire to alleviate the pain of over-population, to find space, feeding ground...

"You do not seek what is natural, the balance," says Chan. "All life understands this. You do not believe. You will not concede. You do not heed the warnings. Your recklessness induces chaos."

"Oh, no," moans Alexei, holding his stomach as if he's in pain. "Please spare me the pseudo-spiritual bullshit. I get gas." Alexei takes another long pull at his cannister and refrains from commenting any further, much to Chan's relief, I'm sure.

I smile sideways, glancing out at the spires and domes of Harbor Town. It might make a great painting. I think about that.

Although my main function is our new society is in the position of Chaser, I am actually a painter, and was one before I left Earth. I wasn't very good, but I had made a name for myself painting the glittering metallic landscapes of home, Greater Brasilia, the Euro-State, all those mega-cities in all their fantastically elaborate constructions and designs. Remember that one of England, that island city carved in steel like a giant spider's web, reaching for the heavens? Yes, I'm sure you're familiar with me by now...

But my energies had run dry, my life's blood in art seemed

to become static. Nothing seemed worth painting that I could be satisfied with. My work seemed to be missing something, maybe always seemed to be missing something. I hadn't produced anything for years, and when the opportunity came along by government invitation to enlist on the *Humility* flight, I signed up. They wanted me there, at the beginning, to watch it happen all over again, shaping and shifting, a recorder of events as they happened. An historian for posterity, and of course I wrote it all down.

Why not? I shrugged to myself, accepting the fact that my once prestigious career, my passion, had ended. Maybe I'd find a new one. And if not, as least I'd be part of a great adventure.

One drunken evening after work, Chan had once seen one of my earlier works in a corner of my digs. "Rohan, you don't paint what is important," he had remarked. "For instance, what does this structure have to do with anything?"

"We created it. It is aesthetically beautiful."

He shook his head. "But it doesn't move one, and it doesn't compliment the surroundings either, it rather pushes it aside, displaces the natural. The achievement of *wu-wei*, creating harmony by integration with the universal flow, is not depicted here."

I shuddered in misunderstanding. "But surely its aesthetic beauty is as important?"

"You are an artist," he had said fervently. "In tune with the natural energies. You have the eye, my friend. Now, release your *spirit!*"

My comm-link chimes and I answer it, placing my helmet back on in order to hear. I could see Chan wait in deathly silence, sweat beading up on his brows.

"Well?"

I pull off my helmet and make a three-second sideways glance at him.

Alexei moans.

"We've got movement."

* * *

A tall man in military fatigues greets us as our transport docks at the last outpost, the last refuge before the Great Wilderness. He quickly checks our identification tags and scans us through. We replace our helmets and walk through the connection corridor to the outward-bound transport. A group of eight heavily armed men are standing outside by the vehicle. Alexei frowns and walks out the hatch toward them. A man steps forward. They communicate on a closed frequency.

Alexei returns and switches to our channel. "They'll be coming with us," he says.

"Military?" Chan raises an eyebrow.

"Apparently there's been confirmation of a sighting," Alexei replies, not sounding convinced. "Manoi in the hills."

"So we need them?" Chan points.

"Multiple signals," says Alexei. "Apparently it's a herd. We'll need the extra guns."

Chan went silent; his face stone.

I shrug. "Let's go."

* * *

The Wilderness is still vast, unpopulated and untouched. It would be the logical place for any animals to be hiding. If any herds survived the wave upon wave of Chaser onslaught the first three hundred years of occupation brought with it, that is. And within a few decades more the Wilderness would be gone, beaten down by the rapidly advancing mega-cities being build. Anything indigenous that does survive would quickly parish when our atmospheric factories go on-line, pushed along by irritants and seismic detonators to kick-start volcanism.

We had hands for such speedy work because our ship was capable of carrying thousands. Built within the heart of an asteroid from the Belt, we coasted out to Pluto where we rode the quantum wave to our destination. Although we have a large fusion reactor, we only used it upon arrival, when the gravitational field of our destination was close enough to yank us off the wave. Once here, the fusion reactor kicked in and we dropped slowly to our new home.

Thanks to modern advances I, and a few Firsts like me from the original crew, have lived long and healthy lives, and have been able to see and enjoy the progress. Revitalized by technology, I am almost three hundred and ninety, with the vitality of a forty-year old. However as with everything there are limits, and they say they can keep me alive for another fifty years or so, if I'm lucky.

The transport rolls across the slushy, reddish snow at top speed, occasionally skidding as the driver makes a sharp turn or applies the brakes for some reason. Alexei dozes in the back, snoring away and driving Chan crazy with the noise. Every so often Chan turns around and kicks the seat. Alexei mumbles and falls silent for a spell.

The ranking officer we've come to know as Ali orders the vehicle to be stopped at the foothills and we disembark. Alexei yawns, uninterested, and lazily picks up his weapon and follows me out. Chan is already out, scanning the thick sky.

"We'll have to be quick," says Ali. "Storm front moving in. Everyone check your suits, then your buddy's. Okay. Move out." He waves his team on, ignoring us. Alexei glances at me and shakes his head.

"Johnny Gung-ho," he mumbles. "Gotta love 'em."

We go on foot, as we can't drive through the icy slopes, or fly through the peaks at that altitude, as it is always snowing at that height and visibility is near zero. Scanners work, but not fast enough for a pilot to avoid the close needle peaks all around.

We walk in relative silence, guns pointed ahead of us, eyes scanning the thickening smog, and snow beginning to flitter down. An hour passes. The light of day is beginning to wane. Nothing happens.

"Looks like this party could be over before it begins," says Alexei. "And I was hoping to bag a hide for my bedroom wall."

The officer's hand goes up. We stop. He signals for his team to fan out. We do like-wise and I take to the right, Alexei the left, and Chan brings up the middle. The mountain peaks, once looming all around us, are now hidden behind blankets of methane. The snow gets heavier, thicker as it falls.

"The transport's comp says there's something in this area," says Ali.

"I don't see a thing," says Alexei.

Chan moves on up ahead of us and off to the right. Ali signals a watchman.

"This is such bullshit," says Alexei. "Even if we can..." He stops and I could just make out an expression of shock on his face through the fog. "*There!*"

Suddenly there is silence, not even a whisper from the troops. They just hunch down, scanning the low ceiling of cloud. No one seems to move for a very long time.

"Multiple signals," says Ali, checking with the transport comp. "Sporadic, though. Hard to get an accurate number with this interference."

A shadow passes behind a thick curtain of fog, and suddenly the darkening spaces come alive with the red streaks of fire. Shouts and whoops from the troops as they blast their way into the encroaching night. After a few minutes they finally stop. Ali flags down the watchman.

"You get 'em?"

The troop moves forward into the mist. "Yeah, I got 'em," he says, dragging a body down the slope. "Got 'em good, too. Goddamn extremists."

I am choked with disbelief. He is dragging Chan's body.

Ali moves forward, looks down at him, and places a slug through his faceplate and into his head.

"Bloody hell, man," I say, head pounding with rage. "He's dead already. What the hell is all this?"

Ali ignores me. "Keep your eyes peeled. His buddies are out here. There's more where this came from."

Alexei looks hard at me. "His buddies?"

"What's going on?" I say. "I demand an explanation!"

"Screwed him good," says someone. "Bloody infiltrator!"

Laughter.

Alexei moves forward. "Hey, man," he says. "You said jack

shit about shooting people out here. What the hell is this? We're suppose to be hunting."

"We are," Ali sneers.

"The hell we are!" Alexei retorts. "I may be many things but I'm not a killer, man. No way. I'm not doing this. To hell with you!"

"I agree," I say. "You said nothing about this. What about the herd?"

Ali turns to face us, a slight grin perched upon the left side of his face. We soon understand. The implication hits me hard, almost knocks the wind out of me.

I hear my own voice quiver. "You can't do this..."

Ali regards me intensely for the first time. I can feel the hardness of his eyes. "My orders come from the top." He moves closer to me, pokes a gloved finger in my chest. "Of all people *you* should understand."

I grab his finger and twist it away. "Yes I do. And I have no problem defending my team. But I won't do it this way. I won't hunt people. I won't hunt humans."

"Terrorists," Ali sneers.

Although Alexei has no sympathy whatsoever with the Naturalists, and was often downright shitty toward them, toward Chan, he has his limits. I can see he is about to launch himself at Ali. I throw myself in his way.

"Look here," Alexei huffs. "Chan may have been an asshole, but he was no infiltrator! Just a dumb kid, that's all. There's no ambush waiting for us out there. Even if there were it doesn't justify this!"

"I know," I say. "Just cool it!"

Another shadow passes off to the left. The troops repeat the earlier process. But soon there is another shadow, then another, moving, flitting behind blankets of cloud and mist.

Something swoops through the smog. A quick a violent scream, followed by a gurgling sound.

"Aziz? Aziz, is that you?"

"What the hell was that?"

Everyone begins chatting furiously.

"Where's Aziz?"

"I thought he was to my left. I can't see a thing!"

"Stow it away!" Ali yells.

The smog is wrapping around us, tighter, tighter, closing in as the snow comes down. I am sweating in my suit. I can't see a damned thing, and visibility is shrinking as the storm moves in.

A shadow. A quick motion. Another scream. The team begins discharging their weapons in the air, all around. There's an explosion nearby; several of us are almost knocked off our feet. Shout of chaos overtake us.

"Keep an eye out on the person nearest you," says Ali.

I grab Ali's shoulder. "I'm not gonna let you get away with this! A man was murdered!"

"Lieutenant!" he barks. "Lock these two up in the transport."

"What?" says Alexei. "On what charge?"

"Obstruction of the law."

The lieutenant and another man grab us both and begin to pull us back.

"*The law!*"

Shots fly about. I can hear them ringing dully through my helmet. As they drag us down the slopes, the ground begins to vibrate ever so slightly, then builds up, and I can hear a thunderous roar. The sound waves, bouncing through the walls of rock and ice, dislodge the snowdrifts.

"Avalanche!" I yell. As my suit begins to get pelted by snowballs I hit the ground with a "humph" and stay there.

"Son of a bitch!" Alexei shouts.

There is a loud swooshing. That is the last thing I hear. I don't quite remember when it was all over, or how I dug myself out. I must have been out for a time, my tank level is low, and I feel the air turning moist and hot, oxygen thinning to vapors...

I am kneeling upon the snow, pulling at Alexei's hands, his helmet faceplate is smash open. In this deadly atmosphere he had hemorrhaged his lungs out into the snow. The only other body I find is a man whose name I can't recall. I leave him.

The storm is in full swing. I want to make it back to the transport. Long range communications are out, which leads me to assume that the slide has hit the vehicle as well. Maybe there will be air, undamaged tanks...

My head begins to swim as my tank bleeds dry. I crash onto my back and lay disoriented, the world swimming in my head. Then I think I see something, something shadowy, hovering over me, moving swiftly, wispy fingers touching me here and there, almost ghostly.

Something large flickers in my field of vision and I freeze. I manage to get to my feet finally, and I turn to stare it straight in the face.

A manoi, hovering there in the smog, great filmy flesh undulating. But this manoi is large, larger than any manoi I have ever seen...

I must have dropped back to my knees for now I am staring up at it. I lock eyes with it for a long while, neither of us moving against the other. I am entranced in its bulbous eyes of swimming black currents.

I suddenly remember how they'd found Hans...

And they are all there before me, surrounding me, great bodies almost translucent, wispy touches of milky white against the red snow, the dark evening, rippling amidst the cool winds, pushing the smog and cloud about with graceful undulations. Thin filaments waver like streamers in a wind, each touching the other with quick flickering movements. Slow, whispery, they make no move against me, nor any move to retreat from my presence as animals do in the presence of humans. They aren't afraid.

I struggle to work my voice, the see clearly, to breath.

They stay around me for what appears to be several minutes. Then, filaments retracting, they turn around a melt away into the mists. The larger one remains for a moment, then backs off, slowly, and vanishes before my eyes like smoke, spreading out, thinning into the clouds.

The last thing to disappear are its eyes...
* * *

I awake in a quarantine room in the hospital. They say they found me in the transport. Although the power was off-line, the beacon down, they said the zeroed in on some faint signals that seemed to flutter, vanishing and reappearing in the vicinity. Extremist movement. Although they never captured any, or found any of their bodies. Only Chan's...

The doctor is leaning over me and telling me that the woman is looking to speak with me. I nod and she proceeds into the room, followed by some heavily armed men.

"You are Rohan Scott?" she asks. "You knew Chan Soong Lee?"

I answer both questions with a nod, head still not quite right. She hits me with another volley of useless questions. This goes on for some time. I ask her who survived. She stares me straight in the face and says that I am the only survivor, and proceeds with more questions. I decide not to tell her about the manoi, although I hear they have been finally declared extinct.

"Have you ever been in contact with the Naturalists? What do you know about "The Way"?"

I've never known "The Way" to be a violent group.

I shake my head. "Nothing really."

She sniffs and writes something down on a pad.
* * *

After a few days I feel able to move and sit up in bed. I am discharged and escorted to a habitat, not my own, a solitary one. All my stuff has been moved in for me. When I ask about this relocation I get no answer.

I'm not allowed visitors, nor am I allowed to travel beyond the confines of this particular complex. I ask when I can leave. They say that all depends on me. And once in a while the woman returns to ask me more questions.

I browse the few posted news nets that I am allowed to access. There are briefs concerning the rise in extremist terrorism and something about an ambush in the Wilderness. Chan Soong Lee is mentioned a few times, and an extremist group's bid to overthrow the government. There is also no mention of the avalanche, and the nets are peppered with reports of sporadic fighting in the cities. The opposition party has been threatening to side with the extremists. There is a curfew in place.

I've started dabbling with paint again, to kill time. I think it's coming back to me. And maybe I'll be able to show something for it this time.

And sometimes, just sometimes, I can feel the rumblings of the earth beneath me as the distant and newly awakened volcanoes vomit their insides out. Gaia speaking in soft gurgles...

And I think about that manoi staring at me from the clouds, and I could swear that it was seeing something distant and far truer than anything I could see, and that it understood it, lived it, its life energy swirling in constant motion behind those great bulbous eyes...

REPEAT PERFORMANCE

How many times had he been through this? A least a dozen times and it didn't appear to be getting any clearer (much to the author's disappointment). Not to mention the huge headache of a medical bill he'd run up since he started working on this one. The chief began threatening to start charging him for the doctor's fees. "You're gonna bankrupt me, Ray." "All in the line of duty," Ray had replied, as the chief chewed on his cigar with a sour look. "And besides, I'm getting closer."

He'd said that a dozen times before, too. But he was sure of it this time. The chief remarked that he'd better wrap this one up soon, and gave him only three more repeats to do it in, otherwise he'd hand the case over to someone else.

"Trust me," he had said, and headed out the office door.

It was raining in the city, like someone had opened the floodgates of heaven and let the largest ocean in the universe pour down onto the filthy streets. He pulled his coat around him tightly, fixed his hat upon his head and, shoulders hunching, walked the back alleys in an attempt to follow the leads he had picked up the last time, before he'd been scratched.

But all he had was a name. No face. Just a name.

Take it easy on me, Carl, he thought. *And a girl. How about a girl in this version for a change? You know, something big breasted, creamy white thighs, tight dress, kinda cheap.*

(Oh, pleeeease!)

He came to a busy, well-lighted street. People were moving about their night business, umbrellas pointing skyward, rows of multicolored umbrellas going up and down the streets of Chinatown. He stopped at a cross street and looked around.

He brought his wrist up to his mouth and spoke into his watch. "Watson," he said to his partner. "I'm at the main crossroads. Again. So far this version of the story is pretty much the same. Don't see any sign of him yet."

The receiver in his ear crackled and came to life. "He's there. My...er...source said he passed through there just five minutes ago."

Well, Carl? he thought. *Mr Source?*

(*Try Wang's*)

"I think I know where I can find him."

"Right. Be careful."

He snickered. "Trust me. This is the final version, my friend."

(*Humm...*)

He'd been following this case for months, or at least several versions of this silly story. Someone had been paying off Sheffield corporate officials for access to private biological weapons information. Sheffield was the largest private body who was given permission by the government to fund such research. And someone was buying a lot of stock in Sang Enterprises, the Chinese equivalent to Sheffield in Hong Kong. The trail of this unknown man led back to Chinatown, to the Chinese underground. Some mafia thug was gonna make a killing of this should Sang gain the advantage, make a breakthrough, and announce it first. Find that man and ten to one you've found the group paying off the officials.

And he was *this* close. This close to finding him or getting waxed again. The answer was just the flip of a coin away. (*Now where is that coin?*)

"Ah, Wang's," he said to himself. "There you are." He walked across the street and over to the entertainment bar. When he got inside he seated himself at the bar by a Caucasian man in a cheap suit, wiping glasses. Ray took out a slip of paper and handed it over to the guy.

"Know this fella?" he asked. "Short man, greasy hair, no balls."

The man regarded Ray with twisted lip, read the name and returned his attention to his task.

Ray grabbed the man's shoulder. "I asked you a question, pal."

The man looked back at him. "Never seen him. Take a hike."

Ray leaned into the man's face. "Is your liquor license expired? I think it has."

The man hesitated, then snapped his fingers. A woman came over, oozed herself all over him.

Now this is more like it, he thought. *Finally, a leggy blonde. I take it those torpedoes are real. Except for the dress, you got it just right.*

(*Yeah, well, enjoy.*)

She pouted and said, "I'll take him in back," her voice was peaches and ice cream, "show him we're all copasetic."

Ray smiled and started feeling fizzy all over. The man grunted.

The lady clung to his arm. "I'm Dee," she oozed. "Dee Delicious."

I bet you are, he thought. He sighed with satisfaction and gave himself a mental high-five.

I owe you one, man, he thought, glancing at the ceiling.

(*Uh-huh.*)

He entered the back room, girl in arm, through a bead curtain to face a small man counting money on a table. Short, greasy hair, nervous twitch...

Oh, not now. Dee, me, I thought we were gonna...I want to... Well just look at her! Give me a break, man. Does this story get any better?

(*Uh...*)

"Johnny the Kid," Ray said reluctantly, going with the flow. "I should have known I'd find you here. How long has it been since I last put you away? Six months?"

Johnny fidgeted nervously. "Actually, it's eight."

Ray shrugged his shoulders. "So who's counting?"

"Me. What do you want, Ray. Whatever it is, I assure you I know nothing about it."

"That's what you said the last time," said Ray. "And the last, and the last, and the last. Do you really expect me to believe you, Kid? Hum?"

"Uh, yeah." His eyes were beginning to shift around the room.

"Who is Chang Lee and where can I find him?"

"Don't know what you're talking about."

He was getting impatient. Dee was looking too good. "Look, son, the story goes like this," he said. "There's a man whose buying stock in Sang like it's the latest designer drug. You work for him, among others, launder money, sell dope, do a little time, and basically know everything I need to know to end this sorry excuse for a story. Now think hard!"

"Who'd want to read a story about bio-weapons and cloning, anyway?"

"Just say the line," Ray pushed.

"Sssssorry," Johnny said, stuttering, waiting for the beating he knew was going to come. "Can't help you."

Ray wrenched his arm free from Dee, flipped the table over. Johnny's hands went up.

"Johnny, my man," said Ray between his teeth. "You're not just gonna let me hang like this are you? In this twenty-first century bomb of a story? After all we've been through? And been through. And been through..."

"Look, man, I don't know," he said, breathing heavily. "I've never met him. No one has."

Ray could smell the alcohol on him like cheap cologne. "I though you said you didn't know him."

"My memory is pretty good under stress," he replied, trying to smile. "Sorry. Too many rewrites, you know?"

Yeah, Ray knew. He looked at the money, now scattered around the room. "You look to be doing pretty well for yourself here. How's tax evasion sound to you?"

Johnny's eyes widened. "No, man, don't do that to me. I'm your best friend. No Johnny, no information."

Ray laughed. "You're information always turns out to be only half right, and I always end up on the short end of the stick." He grabbed Johnny, slammed him against the wall; Johnny coughed for air. "I want the full story this time, starting with Lee."

The lady began pouting again, saddled up to him, said in a baby voice, "All this bad, bad talk. The only things that's bad around here is me." She stroked his crotch. He saw the kinky expression on her face and her glancing at Johnny.

"No, you don't mean..." He wanted to gag. "Can we leave him outta this? Later we can blow this joint and..."

Ray froze as he saw the new look in her eyes, and didn't need to ask to know what was coming his way. He couldn't believe it. Again. Her hand squeezed him like a lemon.

And as he screeched, he never thought that as a soprano he would sound so good...

He woke up to a pretty blonde nurse hovering over him, asking him over and over again if he knew his name. He nodded with stiffness in his neck, images flashing through his head. It was all coming back to him now. His address, his profession, who his girlfriend of the month was, the chief, the case, everything. And especially the case.

Right, he said to himself, stretching the stiffness out of his new body. *Clone number eight.*

Watson floated into the room, glowing a deep shade of blue for disgust.

"How do you feel?"

Ray thought about it for a second, feeling every part of his new self. "On the whole I'd say pretty good."

"Great, because the chief is gonna tear you apart."

"Naw," said Ray. "He loves me like a son."

"You are his son."

"Oh, uh, right." He didn't remember that one. Something must have gotten lost in the rewrite.

Watson shook his metallic torso in disbelief and said, "How many times do you have to die before you solve this case, Ray? Other twenty-first century detectives can usually get by on two or three repeats, and you're certainly not making daddy-O proud."

"Other detectives don't have *this* amateur to deal with." He cocked his thumb at the ceiling. "But I think I've got it this time. Don't worry."

Watson dismissed him and said, "How many times have I heard that one?"

"No, really," said Ray. "Lee must have guessed my move, needed time to vacate his backstreet offices." He scratched his head. "Dee was a decoy. I need Johnny. He's laundering Lee's dirty money. Find Johnny and we can find Lee. Simple."

"Have you ever considered another line of work?"

Ray looked puzzled. "Of course not." He looked up at some point in the ceiling, thought about the way this story had been going. And going. *Have you ever considered another line of work?*

(*!!!!!!*)

"This had better be good, Ray." Watson leaned into his face. "The chief is having a fit. You'd better be right about this."

Ray thought about his lead, Johnny, and where he'd gone wrong in his thinking. But whatever it was, it wouldn't happen again. Not this time. Carl wouldn't go for *nine*, would he? This was all getting rather tedious, right? No one would go for nine. He'd bet his life on it.

"Trust me," he said.

WILDFLOWER

When the bough breaks...

Karlyn ano-Kerr grips the interface around her head with heated disgust. Synapsis are breaking down, some are shifting their pulse rhythms, others are stuck in flux, millions upon millions of nanos are running around, clueless, as if zapped by a heavy dose of the stupids.

She can't understand it; the rooting had been flawless, the bio-programmers for Beta habitat integrated without rejection from the aboriginal millifibers and coaxed by their artificial programmers to grow natural habitats, enclosed and self-sufficient. It had been a textbook performance.

Then why is it collapsing? she chides the static-ridden threshold. Why? Why? *Why?!*

Karlyn writhes in her seat in the control bubble of the landing bug and seethes at the decay of her beloved systems control ganglia. Her program buoy shudders. Algorithms manifest themselves and scatter past her like so many dead leaves on a Veronian wind burst. The leaves brush past her; the massive tangle of information before her strikes a discordant note. She doesn't need this now. Another failure.

From orbit, Cruz des-Manas is running cross-checks on the System Platform's induction flow and stabilization subroutines. She sees him in the digilandscape distance. He appears as an octopus whose many tentacles flicker about at what looks like a swarm of large black flies. Beta is collapsing in upon itself.

"Systems are shutting down all over," says Cruz. "Keep your eyes open. I suspect a possible leak over to the remaining ground systems."

"My program buoy is sinking," Karlyn whines. Her frustration begins to sting. She had sent out for a pattern trace, but so far no luck. The nanopolice had staggered back, babbling incoherently. She huffs. The surroundings become hazy, as if a sheen of ice has formed over an invisible glass window before her. The effect warps the landscape and things appear milky, distant, unclear.

"Organiform supports are dying," announces Cruz. "Hold on the final coding sequence for the nodules. Karlyn, rig to reboot."

"I know!" She sets up the program again. "No dice," she says. "She's sinkin' fast!"

"Recommend we cut contact with Beta. Avoid possible contamination."

Beta is not the only thing sinking, she thinks, as her stomach hits her lap. Whatever's the problem, she's sure it's her fault.

As she prepares to invoke the nanocrobe buffers to coat and isolate the undamaged programmers, a lightning crack ruptures the digisky above. Beta Platform, whose garbled double-speak has dominated most of her interchannels, howls and discharges a static burst.

With quick efficiency her biolastic suit's response mode kicks in. A silver screen goes up, catches the burst, amplifies it and sends it right back at the Platform. There is a shower of blue-white particles, a wrenching noise that threatens to shatter her ears. Suddenly she is thrown clear, and the digivisor on her interface pulls back like melted plastic and withers.

She sits in her organiform chair, head aching, and curses Beta's bloody haemoglobular flow.

"And that, as they say, is that," says Cruz. "I'll check our backups. If this happens again we're gonna have problems growing the colonists."

"Yes, I'm fine, thank you!" she blurts. "Agh!" Her suit is peeling, the heat from the breakdown beginning to burn her skin. She works frantically and manages to pull it off. It crinkles up on the floor and turns from metallic grey to deep black.

"Something must have gotten through to my buoy. My suit has disintegrated."

"Just the overload burst. I'll grow you another."

"'*Just the overload burst*,'" she mimics. "I got fried, Cruz!"

"I know. I can't scan you without an interface suit, though. Check with medical, please."

She sinks back into the chair, careful of her burns. Not exactly the response she's looking for. But then what did she expect? She grunts (*intolerable little shit!*) and wonders what the hell she ever saw in him.

"How's the stock?" she asks. As planet-fall coordinator and bio-farmer she needs to know that the colonists for this particular drop are unharmed. It has taken over sixteen stops this time to find a suitable host-planet, one with an eco-system from which their nanos can grow the living habitats, like the ship grows her a terrestrial body for ground work. Diversity of terrestrial biologicals is not necessary, even a small eco-system will do.

"Organiform nodules seem undamaged. Although I can't get a proper signal from its grid. If we can't verify its authenticity, we'll have to consider the stock contaminated. In which case, as resident biofarmer, I'll need your signature on the liability forms."

Her heart froze. This is not what she was anticipating. She's never lost stock before. Never. Liability forms? Had it come to this for her already? Why not? She had already felt the slow process of marginalization creeping about her months ago. "You could be wrong, Cruz."

"And what would you have me do? Start up the sequence? If there is even a slight chance of contamination, bringing them to life could be the cruellest thing we could do."

"I want a thorough check, and a second opinion. I'm not convinced," she says.

"Well luckily you don't have to be."

"Wrong," she replies. "We are in disagreement, and so protocol demands third party inquest."

"Just a minute, please--"

"You need me to be in full agreement with you on all and any aspects concerning the possible loss of stock. And I call for direct committee intervention."

All department heads and their lieutenants sit on the committee. That is Cruz and herself. But they will both be excluded from the voting process, as they can't be seen as being unbiased. A conflict of interest in regard to the greater good.

"We both *know* that will take time. Time we don't have. Karlyn," he says in a low and even tone, leaning his round face into the camera, "stop fighting me." He's tired of fighting her. He's always fighting her.

"Already lodged and received," she spits out.

"Great."

"I'm gonna run a diagnostic," she insists. "A direct interface with its grid."

He sighs in resignation. "Knock yourself out."

"Grow me another suit. I'll schedule a walk as soon as it is ready."

"Sure. But first let's run through the information on Beta's failure." Cruz begins rerunning the recorded data. "Funny. It shouldn't be doing that!" he says to himself.

"Should take about five hours for the suit to be ready. Right?"

Milky ice crystals now form on the bubble as the sun sinks fast, smudging the view, producing an eerie, cloudy-white glow.

"Isolating pattern buffers," he continues, then mumbles: "It shouldn't do that!"

"I'll be down in medical if you need me."

She looks up through the bubble transparency and notices a group of humanoid aboriginals, squatting in the brush and tall flower-trees nearby. Some fondle with a loving fascination the twisted bits of biohabitat, supports bent in upon themselves, tips blackened, then turn to stroke each others faces with a slow, deliberate caressing, as they always do.

"Sixty percent corruption of Beta's data," he continues. "Still might be able to save it."

A handful of the little hominids are watching her, now. Childishly, she sticks her tongue out at them.

"Karlyn, isolate the induction flow subroutines. We're gonna need...Always intrigued by bloody mud crawlers...Hey! Do you hear what I'm saying?"

"Clear as ice," she snaps, getting up, and flips her camera the finger.

* * *

The first sign that something was going down came when Beta's AI Systems Platform developed a flutter in her bioprogramming matrix. Karlyn thought it nothing at first, probably a power surge somewhere that shot through the system. Happens. Cruz had let it pass too, so even he had thought it not worth mentioning. But then it happened four times.

"Don't get to comfortable," says Cruz, voice booming through the bug's speakers. "Find the problem and get back up here."

Karlyn watches the morning sunlight ooze its way through the foliage, like a thick soup. Similarly, her mind oozes through her brain. An after effect of last night's uneven sleep. She can hear the hanging foliage brush against the cloudy transparency in the breeze. A scratching sound, wanting to get in.

"If you think you can do it better, Cruz," she replies, closing the last seal on her new biolastic suit, wincing, as her skin is still a bit raw, "by all means, feel free to join me."

"No thanks. Terrestrial mud crawling is not my idea of a good time. The stench, the filth, bad working conditions, nah!"

This place isn't the only thing that stinks, she thinks sourly as she rubs her eyes, attempting to wipe away the dream that follows her from the bed in medical. In the dream she was in a deep forest, surrounded by flowers, pollen gliding through the air rich in golden sun rays. Nice fairy tale image. Sniffing a bloom, the flower's petals closed around her face, fine tentacles rushed down her throat. She felt like her insides were being ripped out. She awoke with a start, her body burns, throbbing.

She brushes the vision aside and now gets herself a cup of vitajuice from the service kitchen and proceeds to stalk through the empty lower deck to the equipment locker, her bones feeling heavy, her skin tough. It seems like only yesterday that she had been enjoying the ease of one-third gravity in the bioring ship, before climbing into the reconstruction couch and going into stasis to wake up here. Wherever here is...

She touches a panel and the locker door melts away. She stares at the untidy shelves.

...and to wake up here. With *him*. It never stops surprising her that she had renewed her work contract. Especially when he had been made supervisor of her beloved farming program. Four hundred years of seeding experience and that asshole gets the big chair. She rolls her eyes in disgust. Committee politics, and he was good at playing the game, his new squeeze toy being the Assistant Chairperson. Her stomach twists with that thought.

Farming has been her life. Now would he dare threaten to take that, too?

She considers the pulse gun, hanging in its display.

Karlyn had renewed her registration of monogamy, too, despite the demise of their affair. She had discovered later that he had never registered as monogamous when they were together. By rights he didn't have too, but he should have informed her out of courtesy at least. Instead, he had let her heart accumulate unfair romantic notions, notions of unity and familial obligations, setting down roots, notions he had no intention of entertaining.

"This is who I am," he had said, after she pleaded for him to reconsider their relationship. "Didn't you know?"

She folded her arms across her chest. "You needed me," she said accusingly. "To get on the committee."

"Karlyn..."

"We never had a chance, did we? Did it mean anything to you? Did I?"

He spoke slowly. "It all means something to me."

She kept to herself for a few weeks, taking time off from her duties. When she returned, six months later, she learned that he had been promoted. So what was she to him, then? Another one of his many partners, for sure. Most likely a stepping stone, she had concluded. And he had left quite a footprint on her back.

And it had all gone downhill from there. And in her self-imposed social solitude, regressive feelings of anger and dejection, spawned from the depths of her wounded heart, began to bubble.

She frowns at the ceiling. "Where's your dedication to the stock?"

"Whose stock? Theirs or ours?"

"Funny. I remember learning that there really isn't much of a difference."

He makes a guttural sound in his throat. "Huddling together in the slime like slugs."

"Maybe mud dwellers like the sense of being grounded to something. Belonging."

"Belonging to what?"

"Oh, I don't know. To each other."

"Let 'em. We're the flowers of the wide open spaces, my dear."

"Wrong analogy," he corrects him, digging through her mess for the equipment, ignoring the weapon on the shelf. "Try bees. Going from stem to stem. No," she says to herself aloud. "Bees have a deep communal system. Wind bursts. Carrying wild new seed to unknown grounds. That might be the type of prosaic, expressive crap you're looking for?"

He sniffs. "You stay down there any longer and I might recommend you for psychological readaptation sessions."

It wouldn't be the first time. Farmers have the usual interview session after every ground assignment. The shock and discomfort of being grounded does involve variations of disorientation and discomfort when adapting to a harsh gravity well, discomfort which can inhibit the usual motor coordination in conjunction with the ability to concentrate, to find her core.

She fumbles getting to the control bubble. She can hear the leg brace machinations purring. The ice crystals melt away in the morning's quick and heavy heat. The distant images wriggle in the melting frost and warp into their proper shapes.

Cruz is still chattering in the background, his voice grating on her ears.

"Yeah, well, thanks for the chit-chat," she blurts.

"Sure, but remember to wash when you're done."

"I'm laughing," she says, flatly.

"Glad I could lighten your day. See you on the uplift." The speakers snap off.

She tries to clear her mind as she heads for the antechamber, a hand running absently over her thigh as the muscles work their strange power.

We interrupt this program...

Karlyn slashes her way through the foliage, her sonic blade perfectly slicing the stalks and thin young trees in half. The humidity hangs in the air like slowly moving vapor clouds. Her digivisor works to keep her faceplate clear as she hacks her way to the clearing and the organiform nodules. Following close behind, as expected, come a swarm of aboriginals, dodging through the thick growth with ease.

She stops, teasing them, and they all stop, holding frozen their positions as if suddenly encased in ice. She moves suddenly, then stops. They do the same. She plays this little game with them for some time.

The curious little hominids had shown up the morning after landing, touching the bug, caressing, as if feeling its every living millifiber. When they had first arrived her initial survey failed to report on other land creatures other than Species One, the "gelatins" (small, soft squirming creatures less than 20 centimeters long that lived high up in the flower-trees, either lain in the flower buds or placed there after birth, seemingly unattended, evidently being feed by them). As the seasons changed, she discovered that Species One was in fact an infant stage of Species Two. After completing their gestation externally, they then venture down to the soil for good.

She had spent some time observing them. She had sat with them, followed them, examined as best she could their close-knit, communal relationships. They appeared non-progressive as there was nothing of unnatural construction around, their villages being close groupings of flower-trees and large leafed bushes which hung in an umbrella shape and provided shelter, as if the vegetation grew to accommodate them. When they slept, she used a nano probe to examine their genetic history, the history of a species unaltered in a billion years. An evolutionary dead end, she had concluded that it was safe to proceed with the seeding.

She bounces over fallen trees, dodges bushes, stops, zig-zags through the growth. Her playful audience is not far behind, imitating, simulating, like a group of over-excited preschool children at playtime.

She makes the clearing and stops to catch her breath. The hominids freeze where they are, looking as if they could go on like this for an hour or so, unfazed.

She feels something's wrong. She looks up.

"Shit on me!"

The Beta habitat, or something resembling it, has sprung up during the night like a wild grouping of jungle vines, twisted and interlocking. Filaments resembling veins wander out across the smooth areas of lattices and giant cylindrical leafy enclosures.

"Shit...on...me," she whispers, and quickly switches channels over to Beta. Although it is mumbling incoherently the Platform's biosystems check out five by five down the line.

Her interface chimes.

Before she knew what she was doing she was standing at the habitat, hand outstretched, rubbing the smooth lattices and snaking branches. At the center sit the nodules in their moldings, undisturbed. The aboriginals follow close behind, but avoid getting too close to the structure. They seem content to sit off at the clearing's edge and watch her.

Her interface clangs.

She has never seen anything like it. Although mutations do occur to a small degree (all dependant on the differences in each planet's particular biology) the sequencers have fail-safe coding to prevent extensive mutations; coding that behaves like dominate genes, intent on preventing any large scale rewriting.

But something broke through. Suddenly she is overwhelmed with fear. The fear of failure. She needs to check the nodules.

Her interface rattles for her attention. She tries to ignore it. His voice from earlier in the day is still echoing in the back of her head. Irritation threatens to multiply with each rattle.

Not now!

She sends the call to her answering service.

* * *

She has been plugged into the drop-grid for no more than five minutes when the short, leathery skinned aboriginals suddenly come swarming over to her, poking their heads around at her, hands probing her body with their little, spidery fingers, pulling at her. One bags on her helmet, another begins tugging at her breast pocket. She brushes the little mud crawlers aside and continues working. The "inside" of the grid looks a bit...well...intoxicated.

She picks up a nodule from the molding and examines it for a second time. And for a second time an aboriginal who had been sitting nearby quietly reaches for her and grips her wrists, softly but firmly, while another takes the nodule from her and places it back in the mold. The hominid lets her go and turns away, again.

She watches this lone alien now as it returns to its rocky perch to sit and watch, a solemn look to its brown face. Its small black eyes search her face with a kind of questioning sadness.

What? she wants to ask it. You don't want me to touch the nodule? Is that it? You don't understand why I touch it? Or is it something else?

They seem to grow bored now and move off a distance to touch each other, encompass each other in their long, skeletal arms, locking in full embrace. Sensory communication? Or simply overly affectionate? She had never been able to establish whether they possessed a true, structured language system. But they did seem to be communicating with each other.

She watches them now. She wishes for communication, the right kind, the soft kind, gentle and soothing, hands moving, skin on skin, motion and rhythm...

She closes her eyes, but can not picture it. Not anymore. She opens her eyes, disheartened.

A group of youths have shaped a giant maroon colored leaf into a bowl, and catch the water dripping off the trees in the humidity. They hand it back and forth between one another. She knew that if she drank some, it would taste sweet.

* * *

"Just where the hell have you been?"

Karlyn tries several routes in order to reach the main template without success. The nanopolice bounce back at her without any reasonable explanation. Her frustration mounts.

"I've been busy," she says and sighs, looking up at the towering structure before her.

"Busy," he mumbles. Then says: "Well about an hour ago I started receiving a strange pulsing over Beta channel. Thing just came back on-line. All of a sudden. Just like that."

"I know. I'm looking right at it."

"Looking at what?"

"The habitat. It's up and running. Although she's deformed somewhat."

"Are you shitting me?"

She adjusts her biolastic suit's camera eye. "See that?"

He whistles.

"Try boosting the bandwidth. You should be getting a pulsing sound. I'm attempting to hack into the nodules. So far, no luck."

Cruz is stunned, she knows this because for the first time since she could remember he has little or nothing to say.

"Damn it! Damn it, damn it, damn it all!" she shrieks.

"What now?"

"The buffers on the grid just melted," she huffs, millifibers untwisting, silicrobes breaking apart and floating away. "There's no way to tell if the coding sequence has been affected unless we activate it."

"Gee, do you think?" Cruz remarks. "I've been saying that the moment Beta went down. And that hiccup earlier? I've traced the source and it's not in the system. It's from outside."

She scoffs. "Nothing can get in from outside! That's what the filters are for."

"It can if its own coding comes across as a latent paragene, waiting for instructions," he says flatly. "One of the most extreme probabilities, which is probably why we–why *you*--missed it."

Here we go! She puts her fists up and bangs her own helmet several times. *Stupid! Stupid! Stupid!* It was such a remote danger she'd never had the biofilters check for such a problem. Things just went from bad to worse. For her.

You've been waiting for something like this to happen. Haven't you? Little man.

"So what's that, like, a point-five percent probability?" She sits back on her thighs.

"Something like that," says Cruz. "Well it gets better. Every time we booted up to restart, the induction flow flushed the system, and the resulting surge multiplied the paragenes by a factor of three."

"So we inadvertently caused the codes to multiply," she says lamely. "Certainly explains a few things, anyway."

"Like?"

"Platforms themselves are sentient. We know that Beta was contaminated during primary build-up to sentience after landing. While I was poking around in the matrix, I could have...well...I thought..."

"You thought what?"

"Well, I could have sworn the thing giggled!"

"Uh-huh," says Cruz. "Well in the meantime we need to figure out what exactly is in those pseudo-paragenes. And Karlyn..."

Her skin flushes cold, knowingly. "What?"

"We'll have to destroy the stock. I'll need that signature, Karlyn."

She shakes slightly. "I don't concur."

"Well you called a third party inquest," he said. "It's no longer your decision."

Her heart sinks into her stomach. She sees another error made.

You give that little bitch a good one last night? Made it special so to finish what you started? Trying to go all the way up the ranks, Cruz? Need me out of the way, first? My vote which always counts against you? You emptied my life, my career. You want my committee seat empty, too? This might do it for you. Glad I could help.

"You hear? It's not your decision."

She stares at her idle hands, at her trembling fingers, impassively, trapped. Her voice wanders absently from her lips: "I wonder whose, then?"

She watches the little creatures spin around and begin dipping into the forest, disappearing one by one. She watches them go. The solemn one sits for a moment before getting up. It turns to face her and, before vanishing into the dense growth, sticks its tongue out.

And now a word from our sponsors...

The aboriginals are busy gathering water and food, the soft fruits that hang low on the dripping trees. They pass the water bowls and food back down a line toward the larger group that lays huddled with the coming darkness under an umbrella tree, touching each others faces softly while working. The solemn one sits off a ways by the nodules where she had been working for some time, like a solitary watchman.

Cruz has had no luck deciphering any biosequencing the paragenes might contain. The elusive alien life codes that they harbor remain shrouded in confusion. And with the stock's authenticity in question, the committee has made its decision.

"That's funny. My interface is having trouble linking with Beta," Cruz says. "I can't hear her biorhythms."

"Oh?" she whispers to herself.

"Have you downloaded the toxin?"

"Yes," she lies. "Yes, I have."

The moldings have burst into small flower-trees, nodules nested carefully among the large pink petals, waiting for the final coding sequence that would let them begin their new life.

At least they'd have a fair chance, fairer than any stellar dweller could hope, of that she is certain. Roots. Roots from which to grow...

The bug's primer chimes, signaling the craft's readiness for launch. She waits at the hatch, her eyes swallowing the final picture as hard as they could. Gripping the interface controls around her helmet she logs on and links to Beta's digilandscape. The induction flow appears stabile, despite the strange whooping sound it made. The program buoy holds.

This will be her last action as a farmer. With a strange calmness she keys in the final coding sequence from her wrist pad. She strains to hear the biomatrix flutter and hum in her earpiece. At first the algorithms scatter, then twirl like a cyclone. Piece by piece they fall into place, creating a new yet familiar landscape.

With the system fully automated, she disengages the link.

"Platform termination complete?" Cruz asks.

"Termination complete."

Over the distance the solemn one's voice booms a deep throated tune, thick in the air. This is the first time she's ever heard anything like this spring forth from their alien mouths. She finds something alluring about the song, something rich with deep yet obscured meaning. She thinks to hit the recorder, but for no reason known to her she doesn't move. Maybe it doesn't seem important in the greater scheme of things.

I wish you well. Whoever you are. Whoever, whatever you might become. You, who are rooted and set in your lives to come...

She palms the wall panel. The hatch closes like a flower at sunset. She returns her suit and equipment to the locker, folding it neatly, placing the devices correctly in their holding slots, directly beneath that fully loaded pulse gun. She strokes its transparent sheath, fingers tracing the weapon's every curve, eyes locked on the trigger. She grips the gun's handle firmly.

"Countdown begun. Twenty minute ETA," Cruz remarks. "See you soon."

"Yeah," she says, placing the weapon in her belt and covering it with her shirt. "See you real soon."

As night falls hard the condensation on the bubble begins to crystallize. The view becomes hazy, discordant, and her heart feels a strange release, an unwanted wave of contentment filling the void once there.

"System nominal. Run a diagnostic on..."

...And although I know you will not, could not, ever hope to know me, remember me. I, in my envy, shall remember you.

Cruz's voice cracks over the speakers. "Do you hear what I'm saying?"

"Clear as ice," she says, distantly. "Clear as ice."

ERASE AND REWIND

The distance rumbles with a deep throaty sound as the colors wash over the sky from horizon to horizon. The air shakes and trembles as the kaleidoscope of light rolls in off the One Sea, pushed along by phalanx after phalanx of waves. And I can feel it, the air vibrating against my face, the smell of salt in my nose, the rustle of sand on the beach in my ears as the image pulls into alignment, defines, clarifies.

I look out over the sea, yellow sun coming down from the zenith; it's red dwarf companion already kissing the horizon and melting blood red. I don't bother searching around, I know He is here. Even if I can't see Him.

But I see her, staring up at me, near the shore, water licking her heels. She just stares, blank faced, that's all, just stares, no expression. Her cloths, smeared and tattered, blow like an old sail against her tiny, frail form. In her hands is a doll, gripped hard as if someone might take that, too, away from her.

Hello, I say. She just blinks, as if she's looking right through me. I notice a grey streak making its way across the sky behind her. Smoke. I follow its trail to the smoldering city on the far peninsula, just down and across the bay. The ground trembles as air machines zip low over the beachhead we stand on. Bright stars, very near, and a nebulous cloud front, begin to show through the fading blue sky.

You all alone? I ask. Not a sound utters from her parched lips. I don't think she can hear me, but I feel her, empathetically, her warn out nerves, her once confused but now numbed consciousness. Shock is not unusual in a condition like hers. She's seen too much, far too much for one her age. It's tragic but it's true.

Unfortunate. Very, very unfortunate.

Her head twitches ever so slightly. Her eyes change strangely, taking on a lustrous glow of returning emotion as the hammering blow of recognition begins to chip away at her stone exterior.

What is even more unfortunate is that I know it is I, I am the one who did this to her. Or, more accurately, the person whose body I now co-inhabit.

Uh, hello?

I know He's here. Somewhere. Watching. My Mentor.

So this is what it's all about, then? Was it right of me to ask for this, this kind of experience that I might know what it would be like? To be like *them*? And would I have accepted without resignation if I had known what they were like before? Would I have agreed if I had known about the bullet through her father's head, or the way her mother had been tied down, left to linger for long hours as I had my fun with her, before finally blowing a hole through her abdomen? Would I have conceded if I had known that, in my rage at the child's escape, I would run and run and having spotted her in the sand chased her down the length of sun baked beach until she stopped at the water's edge where she stands now, where I stand, waiting to get the nerve to push her head down into the wet sand until she stopped moving and the water came up to drag her, slowly, into the sea? Would I?

Hey. *Hello?*

This is real; all *too* real.

I taste the salt of tears on my parched lips. The man is crying.

Or is it me?

I have come across the ages, across the streams of time, to a dead and forever burning future. One with no hope for escape. And all of them that I have seen have ended this way. Is there not one that turns away from darkness? I ask my unseen Mentor. At first, he gives me no reply.

My first instinct is naturally to run, to halt this journey into madness, a spiraling madness that seems to have no end. The fear of what is going on, what I had done and am about to do, holds my throat like a crazed man's hand, fingers closed tight, choking, heart pounding, temples throbbing.

Why have you left me here in the continuum like this? Is this all you have to show me? Again and again. Is it? Is this what the outside is all about? Madness?

I want to do something to stop the hurt, the blood. But I cannot; I am only a passive observer in time. But I feel every wild emotion, every ounce of flesh held in these hands, from past to future times, the touch of every loving moment, seized or stolen, the ease there is in snapping an arm, crushing a larynx, killing...

And in each leap forward I can see the spiral get larger, reaching out like tentacles, reaching into chaos. The tears continue to flow.

The girl backs up a step, into the water.

I feel the adrenaline pumping, fueling the heat of the war that now rages across ten worlds. But I also feel the man's anguish (buried deep, but it is there) the tormented cries for serenity that threatens to wrench his soul into dementia. I have felt it in all of them. It is a tiny seed, a germ of a seed that springs from the beginning when there was no darkness, a seed that lies within, screaming a muffled scream as it recedes down and away through the corridors of time, pleading with time, pleading. For mercy.

And should someone not answer that call? Should we? We who *can* be merciful?

I think I hear His voice at last.

Jes?

And I want to hold on to that seed, yes, in the name of God, I do. Hold it, let its warm sanity engulf me, hide me from the encroaching imminence of chaos and darkness. Hold on, yes, as I feel some small part of him does too, pull it over him like a blanket, to shield his eyes, block out the memories.

I am stepping forward, toward her...

And I want to block out the memories, the red and black of

an unmerciful universe. I want to erase the horrid lines of time, spewing its stench out into the quantum fibers of space. I want to go back, back to that one calm point, that singularity created for them at the beginning, before the cancerous tentacles were willed to grow, to devour, back before that singularity, that old focal point for all things, was shattered in one quick and ill-conceived moment into a myriad of infinite and horrifying possibilities, into a universe where nothing is fixed, where everything is unsure.

As I have been unsure, as unsure and as scared as any who have come before me. Or after.

Jes?

The landscape fades, the smells dissipate, the sky blurs as the quantum flux shifts me back my place of origin. The last thing I see is her face, that youthful and innocent face, as the man takes one more step forward...

And finally the garden melts into reality, that beautiful, serene example of calm and harmony that I love so much. Maybe that's why I always come here in this body. The small seed of this human's consciousness's own need for serenity reflected in this one, singular place.

Jes?

I sigh in relief as the horrible vision dies away. Yes, my Mentor? I reply.

Do you see? Do you see how they live? Do you understand? And you are scared of the quantum flow? Of course you are scared. Who wouldn't? Having choice, who would choose this? But the right decision does not always come with a bottle of happiness. Learn from them, Jes. Look what they've done with the so-called freedom they think they've won. What have they gained in breaking from the singular world? Death, disease, blasted worlds of fire and rot. If you have learned anything at all about life, the way to live, they way to love, then you will know what to do. You will not become lost in the confusion that comes with the endless spiral of possibilities. You will not allow yourself to be bound in chaos, never knowing peace. Although you stand in a human's body, swayed by human thought, if you truly understand you will not be like *them*.

Yes, I know now the pain, the unbearable horrors of quantum time. I fear the flood waters of darkest evil that would engulf me...

But surely something could be done?

Yes, something could.

The wind rustles through the olive leaves. I try to loose my thoughts in the sound...

I could offer them a choice, just one more amid an uncounted number of choices, if I wanted. Don't they deserve that much? At least another choice? Don't you feel sorry for them? Does your heart not bleed for their sorrow? Would it hurt to give them one more probability, a choice that will take them outside this universe to our own, that final universe in an endless sea of horrid alternatives I have visited, putting an end to the confusion of their quantum lives?

And I know, stuck in that state between universes, between death and life, that I will feel the horrors of discordance and pain for all eternity. That is the price for a new singular world. There can be no turning back.

You might shake your head and say a price too high, my friend. Much too high for the likes of them. We have never known such darkness could exist in beings who have broken from the singularity. They belong out there. Forget about them. Come back home.

I am standing here now, outside the grove of trees, trembling. I can hear the crowds coming, voices mounting as each footstep draws near. And I see him there, leading them, the one who has been my good friend in my visit here My good brother. My brother Judas.

Judas, who has made *his* choice.

"Rabbi," he says, and gives me a kiss.

A STORY OF KINDNESS

You wonder if the Great Ones have abandoned us? If the world is meant to be devoured by the night? Or maybe you wonder if many are meant to go hungry, or to burn slowly from the invisible rays left over from the days of the Great Burning? I can say I am almost certain. Yes. Yes.

I tell you we wander through evil days, my friend. Evil, evil days. But there was a time when a ray of hope shone in the dark. Yes, there was. And I was entrusted to deliver such hope, but it was stolen from me. Stolen, I tell you! Life stolen from me and from us all by beasts, such unruly animals without a shred of decency in their hearts. Such monsters, I tell you, such brutal beasts the likes of which even Hell would fear. Beasts that would just as soon slit your throat in your sleep without an offer of trade, such–

Oh, but I ramble. Forgive me. So sorry. My thoughts have the tendency to possess me, spring to life. You know how it is...

(Ah-hum.)

Ah, that fire is a lovely thing, my friend. Such warmth, lovingly given, lovingly taken, and I thank you for letting me share it with you. I sense such kindness in you, my friend, as is rarely seen in this world. Yes, I do. And I am grateful, but...

Shall I show you what real kindness is? Hum? A trade. Yes? I will trade, trade with you this moral story, my story, my friend, before I continue on my way. And even an old tale can be worth something. Could I interest you in this antique, then? Would you be interested in the ramblings of an old fool? Would you like to hear it then? Yes? Good.

I shall begin when I was younger and roamed the wilds, trading–oh, stories for food mostly, stories of glorious antiquity, when the world was young and alive, and of course some odds and ends, useful things. Let me see...I once stopped off in a little village of bone and ash. So long ago it was, what year anyone can guess, for who has taken note of such things since the Great Fire burned? Ah, these days of anguish...

But I digress.

(Ah-hum.)

Let me see. Yes, a trader I was.

No, no. A bringer of hope in the darkness...

* * *

Yes! Yes! Come forward my wayward friends, come and let me show you something the likes of which you have never seen before. Yes, don't just stand there. Come. You give me five minutes–just five–and I'll show you something worth having. Yes, sir, just for you. For you. And you, my darkly dressed friend. And you too, sir. Yes, yes, no need to push and shove like beastes, come now, there is plenty for everyone. Plenty. We're civilized people here.

Good. That's it. Oh, is the that wrist band gold? Good barter, good barter. You may not wish to part with it now, but just wait until you see what I have in store for you! Useful things, and stories of such adventure. No need to look elsewhere, I guarantee you!

(Ah-hum.)

Yes, I know. Not much of a place, but what is these days? Just a carriage, some wooden walls and a leaky tin roof on rubber wheels. Just big enough for me and my stock. But what a stock! And I want not. No sir. Hey! You there! Stop pushing. Let's be civil, shall we? A little kindness, please. Good.

Now where was I? Ah, yes, who could know that down here at the end of this lonely little street, this cul-de-sac of our little world, could hold such treasure? See here, a rare find! An antique they used to say. Could I interest you in this antique? Of the finest quality, I'm sure. And it's authentic! A canteen they used to call them. Holds a good day's water supply. Much needed when crossing the wastes between the black cities. Yes sir, let me tell *you.*

And these? Yes, good protection against the radiation, they used to say. Just put them over your body. Somewhat heavy but hey, could save you from becoming a sterile wretch. Know what I mean? Of course your do. Hey? Hey? Ha, ha!

Yes, it is a dark time indeed, my friends, and more reason why you should trade for some of these items. Could mean your very survival! I have everything anyone might need here. Yes, sir. Right here. But don't delay, I must be off for the next settlement in two sun-passings. Much joy to spread, yes indeed.

So what will it be, good people? But, of course, what do *you* have? Something for me? A little gold? Some silver, perhaps? Something useful? Remember this is an honest trade. I am doing you a great service, for you and your children.

Review the picture: Deep bronze light filters through the thick, cloudy sky where the children scavenge. *Your* children. In their tatterings they grip at each other, pulling at useful things found in the heaps left behind from the Days of Mania, sometimes with shouts or whines in their mouths. And you sit, perched upon a lone stone wall, a sentinel guarding the pathways, watching for the creatures once your pets, whom you devour, and who now hunt *you* down for eats.

And if it's not the creatures it's your neighbor, stealing from your backyard and slitting your throat. Some even steal children. Can you imagine?

But let me slow down, pace myself here. I can see you're getting tired, agitated. Why don't I begin with a story. Yes! I shall begin with a story. A story for precious minutes of your time, time to browse through my goods. Agreed?

Well I shall begin with a very special story, very special, the holiest of stories. You have not heard of such a tale? No?

You see in the days before the Fire there were windows in every home. Indeed, there were great buildings of windows that reached up to the tip of the sky! But no window before or after can be compared to such a window as the Window of Plenty. Such a special window, a holy window, such light and vision...

You have not heard this one? Well, gather close, my friends.

(Ah-hum.)

And now...

The Dark Wastes, the endless expanse beyond the black cities, holds little but death for us, as we all know. Only when a day has been very kind can one find something useful between the blasted rocks and wind blown sands–if you are brave enough to travel the endless Dark and make it back, that is!

You see, by the Mountains of Time, between the Hills of Yesterday, out on the edge of the Great Empty Lake, I had a home in a village. Not much: a woman, our boy, and a small wooden box to keep out the night. We had enough to live on; breeding cattle-dogs for meals, trading some for water and other things. All was good. We did not want as much as most.

But the virus of the Days of Mania lingers like a specter, just out of sight...

One day a man came to us, from where none of us knew, but he had a dozen or so men with him, all armed, all angry. They shouted at us, and when they didn't feel like shouting their metal pipes shouted for them in great bolts of lightning and with a cracking sound. The man rounded us up like cattle-dog, made us work, built a high fence of needle-wire around the village so none could leave.

He instilled terror in our hearts by killing a few of us often. They were usually the old, who could not work, or those among us who resisted. The pipes would flash and then *crack*! They fell dead like flies. And when that wasn't enough, they began taking our wives and daughters, making us watch with rage in our silent mouths...

One day the man, who called himself "The President," took our son as his slave boy. When he finally took my wife, I protested. So when he was done with her he slit her throat and had me chained and beaten for three days every sunrise; held me in a dark shed for how long I do not know, but I'd almost forgotten the sun and his warmth.

I was broken, you see? Broken. But when I healed and was released I devised a plan and escaped in the dead of night by digging with my bowl, under the ground like a mole, under the fence. And I ran with nothing in my arms or on my back to sustain me.

I ran into the desert and they pursued me with anger in their mouths. So I went into the Dark Wastes where they dared not go, hoping the Great Ones would see me, remember me their child, and take pity.

Well, hope beyond hope, take pity they did! I wandered, perhaps for days, maybe longer, I can not recall as I was ill and near death from lacking. But one day there it was, shining in the forever burning sun, glistening with hope and waiting. Waiting for me.

It stood long and tall in the middle of the hot sun, among the rocks and fallen walls of a deserted and lost village, silent and majestic and holy. I touched it and it shimmered, the glass seemed to ripple in the heat. I looked through, and it showed me things. Great and wonderful things beyond its ancient frame.

I saw a field of green waving in a breeze, with colors on the tips of thin stalks. And I saw many creatures the likes of which I've never seen before. Some even flew through the air! Can you imagine? And there were blue skies. *Blue!* And puffy white clouds, nice and clean and pure.

And each time I touched the glass it shimmered again and changed pictures. I saw a great body of water that stretched to the far horizon; I saw great cities of shining metal, and people, millions upon millions of people, laughing and playing and dining on such fine meals.

And then a thing happened that I could never expect: the ground shook, the glass rippled and seemed to reach out to me, sucking at me–and I fell through! Yes, I fell *through* the Window and into such a place as I could never have imagined. And there were people there, holy people who took care of me as though I were one of their own, and all my needs were granted.

Oh, it was a place of great joy, great hope, where no one was in want and all was provided for. It was a place where brutality did not exist, and peace reigned in the hearts of men.

Such a place brings life back into the soul, and kindness back into the heart. And although I did not want to leave I knew I had to return, so they kissed me and cried and gave me all that I could carry in my arms and on my back. And they bade me share a little bit of that kindness back to you, my brothers and sisters.

Oh, I feel your destitution, my friends, and have sympathy. But I have come back! Come back for your benefit!

Yes, it is true! And I've brought back with me a story of kindness and these precious necessities, to trade and to provide hope. Hope that we may be smiled upon by the Great Ones, as I have been, and find a little bit of that kindness to spread to others that we may rebuild our broken world.

And so...What? No, I had gone back several times before but upon arrival I found the Window gone. Gone, I say. But who knows where it may show up next? In someone's time of need? Yes. But that one time was all that was needed to bring to you hope. Who knows, maybe you may be blessed to come upon it one day, in your own need, to fall through into paradise.

Not a bad story, hey? No, a wonderful story. So keep your eyes sharp for that glitter of glass, that sparkle of salvation, that...Why do you shake your heads at me? Why do you mumble? What are you saying there? You! What is this? Why, I do and say these things for you, and–and what do you hold in your hand?

Get back! What is this? Don't push, there is plenty for all to trade. Wait! We must be civil! We must be like those holy people. We must–you'll knock my carriage over! Wait I tell you! It is true. Your destitution can end, and–don't hit me with that! You monsters, monsters all of you! Stop! Stop I tell you! *Stop!*

Ah-eeee!

* * *

Oh, evil days. Oh, hard pressed and broken bones. All my precious things gone. Gone! My offer of hope, shattered! Gifts of salvation, stolen!

Savages! Undeserving beasts!

Suffering. Great suffering now. Oh, I fear it. Yes. Ah, cruelty. Shall Death come now? Shall night fall hard upon me? Upon all children? Does the heart ever warm? A curse! A curse, I say. We are cursed! What to do, what to do...What are you looking at? Yes, you! You mock me? Laugh at me? You find something funny here? Be gone with you! Be off, I say, you...What?

Oh.

Oh, so sorry. So sorry *indeed*, my friend. Yes, I remember you. Forgive me my wild mind...You have something there. What is it? Something useful, maybe? Yes? A bit of meat from that fire over there? I see you have a kind heart. A very kind heart indeed. Did I say I would show you what *real* kindness is? I did, yes?

Ah...Look here, then, take this piece on my belt for instance. Been around ten thousand years and a day, I was told, back before they built what were called the Eyes in the Sky, or the mechanical beasts of burden, those ancient of ancient days, glorious antiquity. And still in good condition! See the perfection of the blade?

Come closer. Come. That's it. That's right. See? Glistening with hope. Yes, that's it. Hope. Long, shiny, pretty, something *sharp*, yes. That's it! Something sharp and kind, so very, *very* kind. Come closer.

(Ah-hum.)

Here, let me interest you in an antique...

COMPANION

I never knew her name.

I probably never will.

I watched her every day and every night of every year that she lived in the old dwelling, and not once did she ever show any sign of wanting to leave. I felt so bad for the place, it was going to be so lonely without her. She was its companion.

And I was hers.

She never, truly knew it, of course, as I kept my distance from her warm smile, an anonymous companion throughout the years. And in all that time, I never learned her name or where it was she had come from. Somewhere out there, I presumed, and I was very glad to have her here to break the loneliness, so it really didn't matter what she was called.

I called her: Love.

I had heard the thunder crack, saw the bright light, felt the passing warmth as the silver thing she rode in fell hard from the violet sky to smash into the sea. I could feel the life of the thing dying, pulsing its last breaths into the deep waters until it finally ceased being.

Then she came.

Out and onto one of the land masses she dragged herself, a sack of things on her back, pulling off the white, hard shell to expose her beautiful head, working herself out of her white, outer skin.

(Sigh.)

Such beauty like I have never seen.

She was as graceful as any filmy air floater, as lovely as any sunrise; her yellow-sun hair hung about her shoulders and her eyes were as crystal blue as the sea waters in which she swam. The waters were I looked up at her for the first time and sighed and fell in love.

If only she could have seen more clearly, she might have seen me.

Maybe.

I had spent my entire life here, swimming these waters, yet never finding anything in which to spend all that long and dreadful time with. Nothing suited to my mind, anyway, and certainly nothing as beautiful....

In the beginning, I would love to wash up to shore with the waves to gaze at her, watching the large spinning galaxy of light points rise above the ocean horizon as night would quickly fall. Her eyes would glisten with the many lights of the dark sky, and of the galaxy, and she would simply sit there and stare at it, almost in wonder, almost in longing. Then she would get up and walk into the small dwelling she had built with pieces of her dead shiny thing sitting at the bottom of the sea, and rest until morning.

And it would certainly be a long night, waiting....

She spent most of the morning gathering plants she could eat, or fishing out the creatures which lived close to shore. Other times she spent sitting by a box, listening for something, anxiously.

On many lazy afternoons, I was brave enough stretch out my mind to be the tree she sat under or the leaves which played around her feet, touching and running away. I was even in the wind, at times, wrapping my many arms around her and caressing her every curve.

Sometimes I would reach out, stretch my mind to the very edges of her thoughts, pick up

traces of her feelings, her wants, her loneliness. And some days these thoughts were more bitter than others.

She has spent most of her time in the dwelling, sitting by the window or in the small doorway, just watching the sky. I didn't might sharing her with the place, as it let me wander through floor and aching, shiny walls, or the plants or wind she would walk off into, as I would be right there, in an air floater or gazing out at her through the single great eye of a glow-flower. Every night I would whisper my love to her through the open window of her dwelling, softly. She never heard me. Every day I would play about her feet, or hold her in the wind. She never saw me.

For many years we had been happy together. We walked together, swam together, spent every hour of every day and night together and it really didn't matter that she could not see or hear me. The company was all that I craved.

After some time, the loneliness returned to cool my warm days and nights; to rip a dark hole between us which grew larger with each passing of the great spiralling galaxy. Having her there was not enough. I needed more. I wanted her to know I was with her, and that I loved her. I wanted to talk with her, smile with her, laugh with her, sing with her.

In my desperation I shook the trees, tugged at her feet through the leaves, grabbed at her in the wind. I jumped on the dwelling, rattled the shiny walls, yelled at her through the open window.

All day. All night.

And, finally, I dared to foam and splatter my way out of the water, up the beachhead.

She didn't come out.

In my frustration, I ran back to the isolation of the cool sea waters. There I stayed for many days, bathing my hurt in the chilly depths.

When I finally returned some time later she was gone. The land before the sea was empty, as it had been for many passings of the sun before. It was alone. I was alone. Again.

For many days afterwards I would look through the eye of a glow flower, visit the tree where she often laid her perfect form, ran with the leaves through the land, blew through the wind, but she was not there.

Come back!

She never did.

I only wander as far as the shore now, and then I turn around and head back out into the cool, deep sea waters to bury myself in the thick, muddy bottom. Alone.

The many years Love and I spent together seemed like a brief moment, but they were the happiest years I can remember.

I never knew her name.

I probably never will.

THE INVISIBLE WAR

Scene: scroll image 333-453321-33a. Camera quickly pans to a wide shot of a far wall. Image shifts back and forth, tilts fifteen degrees, shoots up toward the high ceiling. Halo fuzz around the distant white light, then down to look at a pair of hands, palms open. **Enhance.**

He sits on the hard floor of this prison cell because he's been denied a chair, a table, a bed, anything of any comfort at all. A dim light burns in the center of the room, suspended from a high ceiling. Morning has long since broken, and they've denied him a meal for the third time. He picks at pieces of food left over from the other night, trying to make it last.

He knows he should be frightened as he sits in their prison, terrified, for in a few hours they are going to execute him--again. But oddly enough he feels a strange calm, like cool waters upon a placid lake. He sits, expectantly, shuffling sounds crawling behind that steel door...

***

Scene: scroll image 333-443320-12a. **Playback.** *Camera pans back and focuses on a beachfront, water at low tide. Audio picks up voices. Camera moves in to get a shot. A woman moves into the frame.* **Enhance.**

Karyn's yellow, sun-bleached hair wraps around her neck in the wind like a scarf. A baggy uniform does little to mask the curves and softness he knows are under there, had felt the night before, wants to feel again.

"Council has ended deliberations," she says, forcing a small smile. "Jon."

He nods gravely and looks at the deep well of sky, at the stars coming out now against the fading blue. They point at him, as if accusing him of some dark tragedy. He winces.

"I see," he says flatly, not so much to her as to the sky.

Off in the distance, by the now sleepy shore, the remnants of the city stretch, charred, broken, in ruin yet still used. He can just make out the thin smoke columns of fires, burning steady against the rising evening wind.

 He sucks it in, the wind, lets it caress his face this one last time before he must give it all up to the Dhijad, the wind, water, sands of his homeworld. He curses his artificial eyes for the clarity of memories.

"I suppose the order comes effective immediately," he says going through the motions, knowing the answer.

"Yes," Karyn replies. "The transports have already begun the evacuation." She walks over and places her hands on his shoulders. "The clans are in unison, Jon. There is no other choice, of that we all agree. The eco-system is all but destroyed, the ozone has been burned away, the water unfit to drink..." she stops. "We only have a short time to make the escape window."

A bird cries overhead. He considers it for a moment.

"And so we fall back again," he mutters to himself. "Oh, if you only knew the *truth*!"

Karyn continues, unhearing, his words falling off her like leaves. She brushes a hand over his face and meets his eyes with a look of quiet longing. "There's plenty of time left," she says. "I'll be leading the first fleet away from Lyra at mid-sun tomorrow." She pushes her softness into him. "Your favorite dinner is waiting," she whispers. "And more. Let's make it last."

***

Scene: scroll image 333-443320-12b. Shadows and silhouettes of ruins scatter the view of the shore. Double moonlight casts double shadows, blankets rustle. **Enhance.**

The memory of Lyra is now haunted for him, and there is something, something he can't explain that laments the city's broken back, the voices echoing into the night where only the spirits of the dead now wander. He can feel it in his heart and in his bones, a swirling band of sadness and peace, as elusive as the evening mist, yet as perceptible as a fever.

Fires twinkle in the city below, while the stars shine hard and silent like sentinels in the sky. He can hear the water licking at the shore, the thrum of a vehicle down a dark and narrow street. The air seems pensive. How long now? How long would it be before they come? This time he tries not to remember....

Karyn shovels a fork full of leftovers into her mouth from a plate near their makeshift bed. The candles still burning and wiggling in the moving air, casting an eerie glow and producing quick shapes his eyes could hardly record properly.

He can hear them, his eyes, their tiny machinery whining and clicking in his sockets.

Karyn lies flat on her stomach, her legs entwined in his, the plate on the floor. "The last time I will see these stars with you," she says, eyes fixed up, her back to him. "And then we'll meet at Point Ryaan..."

He smiles inwardly. "Why don't we take the boat out tonight, into the harbor? You and me under these stars?" He'd always secretly wanted to, that night, to let it all slip away, fall behind him as if he'd never been a part of it. The Great Burning.

She carries on as if he hadn't said a word. She sat up, and he saw the smooth skin of her back, reached out and touched it.

"Karyn..." he breaks off.

She turned to him, soft eyes betraying concern. "Why do you do this to yourself?"

"I don't know," he says, wanting to pull the eyes out of his head; the eyes *they* had given him. But his brain remembers as well as his eyes. "I guess I expect to rewrite it all. Or to push delete and wipe the sad song Lyra plays away."

"Everything must play itself out," she says. "Just as it should."

"Should it?"

She smiles somewhat wickedly. "Just for you, Jon."

Her face resumes the composure it had before, before the shift in conversation, the way it had been that night. She gets up, the blankets rustle down, exposing her flesh to the moonlight, cold and pale and ghostly. She walks to the window. She glances back over her shoulder, eyes hard, accusing.

"Karyn, I wanted to tell you...I wanted to say..."

He closes his eyes and keeps them shut. But he can never keep them shut for long.

***

Scene interrupt. Scroll image 333-443320-12c. **Playback**.

He hears the boats rocking in the docks, the soft groaning of the hulls in his ears. He opens his eyes. The water glows silver in the pale light of the moons in the crystal sky. He sees her form on the quay, silhouetted and haloed in a ghostly moonlit aura.

And he can feel them out there, hidden behind the velvet of night, ready to come bursting forth from the quantum bubble and set fire to the night.

He shivered. He had been there, on Perigrine, when they'd come, set fire to it, watched it burn. And he'd seen Carrion reduced to ash and steam from a distance as the clan ships hurtled away from the bloody massacre.

But he was supposed to help stop it, stop it all. Wasn't he?

The knowledge of his course of actions came to him the day the Dhijadians had knocked out Skylight Station. His homeworld to be spared by surrender. And it would be the only way to stop the advance, wouldn't it? To give in? To give it up to *them*, to fall back into the Realm from which his people had come? That's what they wanted, isn't it? The Dhijads. That's what they used him for. Right?

He squeezes his eyes shut and shakes his head. (*Scene interrupt...*) He opens them, wet, glossy, tired. So very tired. (*Scene continue...*)

"I know we don't deserve a second chance," she says, "after our failure here...But the people of Point Ryaan seem content enough to let some of us settle there."

He suddenly grows cold, shivering. "Karyn," he says. "I want to hear you say it."

"They've allocated a large portion of the southern continent for resettlement," she continues. "A grand gesture even for them."

"Kayrn." His heart pounds. The moment is fading.

"It would be nice," she says, her smile distant in the moonlight. "To finally stay somewhere together. You. Me."

"I need you to say it."

"I've got a little secret," she said, smiling mischievously. "Want to hear it?"

"Oh God, please say it!"

"I've bought a little place by the shore on the peninsula for us," she says. There is a crashing in his brain. "Just for us. You like the sea, the boats." She reaches out for him to join her on the quay like he should, like he had done that night before they had come, unannounced, known only to him, through Lyra's defences, known to *them* through his eyes...

"My gift to you, Jon," she says.

He quivers slightly and remains where he is, takes a long, deep breath and awaits the inevitable, the lightning crashing to earth. Again.

"Goodbye, Karyn," he says.

She doesn't hear. She watches the stars.

But he swears, swears that this time as she looks back, hand still outstretched, before the night becomes day and the water in the bay boils and the little shanty town built upon the ruins blows away in the fire wind, that she is smiling at him. Smiling.

And he waits for the scene to fade, for the vision to smudge and swirl into base colors and finally turn black.

Through the playback he can hear shuffling sounds behind that steel door...

And he waits, longingly, in the dim light for that promised peace that seems to never come, that final resting peace where at long last he can relinquish countless hours of playback.

Peace.

The peace of the dead.

Carl Rafala was born in Connecticut in 1970. He earned his BA in English from Albertus Magnus College, and then spent the next five and a half years in South Africa. He then earned his MA from the internationally renowned University of South Africa in 2000; his dissertation was an intertextual dialogue between the Homeric Epic and the science fiction text.

Having written for most of his life, Rafala finally got around to sending his work out, subsequently finding publication in small presses by the end of the 1990s. He has taught Freshman English at Quinnipiac University. This is the first collection of his work.

ABOUT GREATUNPUBLISHED.COM

greatunpublished.com is a website that exists to serve writers and readers, and remove some of the commercial barriers between them. When you purchase a greatunpublished.com title, whether you receive it in electronic form or in a paperback volume or as a signed copy of the author's manuscript, you can be assured that the author is receiving a majority of the post-production revenue. Writers who join greatunpublished.com support the site and its marketing efforts with a per-title fee, and a portion of the site's share of profits are channeled into literacy programs.

So by purchasing this title from greatunpublished.com, you are helping to revolutionize the publishing industry for the benefit of writers and readers.
And for this we thank you.